The Other Side Of The River

By

Charles E. Gist

© 2002 by Charles E. Gist. All rights reserved.

No part of this book may be reproduced, stored in a retrieval system, or transmitted by any means, electronic, mechanical, photocopying, recording, or otherwise, without written permission from the author.

ISBN: 1-4033-3789-6 (Electronic)
ISBN: 1-4033-3790-X (Softcover)
ISBN: 1-4033-3791-8 (Hardcover)

This book is printed on acid free paper.

1stBooks – rev. 05/18/02

Any characters in this book, which resemble any person living or dead is purely coincidental. They are all a product of the author's imagination. This book was not written to be offensive to anyone. It is for enjoyment only. Let's hope it serves that purpose. I would like to thank Rick and Christy Fox for their editing and typing.

Charles E. Gist

The old man in the following story was fed up with the way that the history of the War for Southern Independence was being taught to the people of America. It just didn't seem important to people anymore. Heritage was a thing of the past and most everyone had just as soon it stay that way.

The further he looked into the future the worse it got. He finally stood it as long as he could so he decided it was time to try and do something about it.

Through his visits to a boy beginning in the year 2065 he would make his attempt not to change history, but to prevent the total annihilation of the memory of the Confederacy. He had fought for four long years to try and preserve it. So what difference would a few more years of service to the cause matter?

We pick up at the occasion of the old man's second visit to the boy and the adventure begins...

Chapter One

A movement at the foot of his bed suddenly awakened Johnny. He raised up and looked and there stood the same old man who had appeared to him previously.

"Hello, Johnny. How ya been doing?" the old man inquired. Johnny caught his breath and said apprehensively, "Whew, you scared me there for a minute. I didn't think I would ever see you again."

"You probably wouldn't have but it got to bothering me when I overheard the conversation you and your pa had during my last visit. I just couldn't leave things the way they were. I had to come back and try to explain a few things to ya."

"Well, I sure am glad to see you came back, cause there sure are a lot of things that I didn't understand. Why don't you pull up a chair and sit down? Would you care for something to eat or drink?"

"Naw, I don't eat and drink much anymore. Not like I used to. It'll be fine just to sit here and rest and talk. You know the last time I was here, Johnny, you said they told you in school that the War for Southern Independence, or the Civil War as some people prefer to call it, never occurred."

Charles E. Gist

"Yeah, that's what the teacher said and he also said he didn't wanna hear anymore about it or he would have to report me to the proper authorities 'cause it was all just a myth that a bunch of southern people got together and made up anyway."

"Yeah, I remember, Johnny. But I'm here to tell ya if you don't believe anything else that you hear or see in this world, that ain't the truth. And I'm gonna prove it to ya. 'Cause you see, I was there through four long years of fighting and I know what went on. If that's a myth, it sure is the roughest one I've ever had to live through. You see, Johnny, there was a Great War in the years of 1861-1865 between the northern states and the southern states. The northern states' president was Abraham Lincoln, who was from Illinois, and the president of the southern states was Jefferson Davis, who was an ex-United States Senator from the state of Mississippi."

"What was this war all about?" Johnny asked.

"It's kinda hard to explain. Some people say it was fought over slavery. That's where the people in the south used the black people from Africa to do all the work. But that's not all quite true. They were a lot of slaves in the northern states too. Most of the slaves were sold to the people in the south to work on their plantations and raise cotton and other things by the rich people in the north. Now that wasn't the only reason for the war. There was a lot of economic and political reasons why the War for Southern Independence was fought."

Johnny tried to conceal a yawn.

"Look, it's getting late, Johnny, so I think I'd better go for now so you can get some sleep. I'll come on back later and talk to you some more."

"No, don't leave. I want to hear all about what you've been telling me. I'm not really sleepy anyway."

"There's still a whole bunch of stuff I gotta tell ya, Johnny, and I can't do it all in one night. You know you have got to get your rest if you ever want to grow up and make something out of yourself. I sure wouldn't want to be the blame of your getting sick or something. So you just go on and go to sleep, don't worry too much about it right now. I'll be back." The old man got up, patted Johnny on the head and walked through the door.

Johnny lay in his bed with thoughts and questions going through his head. He didn't think he would ever get to go to sleep. Eventually, exhaustion overtook his body and he slowly fell into a restless sleep sometime in the early hours of the morning.

Johnny had formed the opinion that the old man was telling him tall tales. But he still looked forward to his return.

A few weeks went by and finally the old man returned and continued what he termed as Johnny's "enrichment of the mind." He knew Johnny was unaware that he was destined for great things in the future.

"You know what I've told you, Johnny, is only part of the reasons for the war. Why, they're just too numerous to count. And I sure don't claim to know all of them. I can only tell you from my own point of view and what I seen with my own eyes and what other people told me. Anyway, when I joined up with the Virginia State Militia, we went marching off to war to kill those Yankees and protect our rights and homes. Let me tell ya, we sure was a gay and happy bunch. The band was playing marching music, the ladies were cheering and throwing flowers. Course a lot of 'em were crying."

Johnny looked puzzled so the old man asked, "Whatcha looking so confused about, son?"

The Other Side of the River

"Well, you said you were a gay and happy bunch, no wonder the women were cheering."

The old man said, "I don't understand what you're talking about Johnny."

"Well, you mean to tell me that every one of you was gay?"

"Sure, we were happy to be able to go and shoot Yankees before it all got over with."

"What's that got to do with none of you liking women?" Johnny asked.

The old man scratched his head and said, "Now, you listen here young feller. There weren't none of us boys that didn't like women as far as I know. I don't know where you ever got a notion like that."

"Well, you were the one who said you were gay and that means that you don't care for women doesn't it?"

"Not where I come from," the old man said. "All that means is that we were happy and having a good time. You know, enjoying ourselves. And if you keep this up, I'll have to go and find me someone else to haunt."

Johnny said, "No, don't do that, I didn't mean anything by it. I guess it must just be a different meaning of words for different times or something. But you sure had me worried there for a minute. I sure wouldn't want to be bothered by a funny ghost."

"Well, you sure don't have to worry 'bout that and if you don't mind, I'd like to get back to my story. Anyway, everybody wanted to go to the war. Some of the boys 9 and 10 years old wanted to join up, but of course their ma's wouldn't let 'em. I even seen a few old men who had to be at least 80 trying to volunteer. Course we didn't need them either, 'cause they was plenty of people in between those ages that was willing to fight. But we all thought that at that time that if we give those Yankees one good whipping it would all be over with anyway. Everybody knew that one good southerner could whip at least five Yankees.

Most of us was as green as grass and didn't know anything about soldiering, but we were raised up around guns, so we could all shoot pretty good. Didn't take too long to figure out that shooting wasn't the only thing that it took to make a soldier. Can you imagine a bunch of ol' farm boys trying to learn how to march in formation? They sure did have some fancy maneuvers. Marching along there you might hear the order, "right shoulder shift". Heck, some of us didn't know our right shoulder from our left foot. I told the sergeant this, but he didn't seem too amused. So, I figured I better keep my mouth shut.

After a while, we did learn a little bit of it, but we never did get real good at all that fancy stuff and we figured we didn't need it anyway, seeing' we'd all be going home in about two or three months at the most."

"Are you sure you're not making all this up? Mom and Dad always said I had a wild imagination, but I'm not so sure you don't have me beat."

"No, Johnny, I'm not making all this up. Sometimes, I wished I was. But it's the gospel truth, every word I'm telling ya."

"Well, I don't know whether I ought to believe you or not. As far as I know you aren't even real. And if you are or was or whatever, you've never even told me your name."

"Can't say as I can much blame ya, Johnny. After all, it just seems that for some reason or the other people just haven't been taught the true history of what went on in this here country of ours. So, please forgive me for not introducing myself. Like I told ya before, it's been a long time since I had a chance to sit down and talk to someone and I guess I must've clean forgot all my manners. My name is James Williamson Phillips. I

Charles E. Gist

was born on February 18, 1843 in Maury County, Tennessee. My parents were John Carnally Phillips and Mary Jane Williamson Phillips. I was their third child. I had an older brother and an older sister."

"If you was born in 1843, then what in the world are you doing here? Don't you know this is 2065? There just ain't no way anybody could live that long."

"You're right, Johnny. There ain't no way that anybody could live that long. But for some reason unknown to me, I was selected to come here and talk to you. I think it was through the process of elimination. You see, General Lee was too busy and Jeff Davis was down with the influenza or something, so they decided to send me instead."

"Why would anyone want to send someone two hundred years out of their way just to talk to one person?"

"You see, Johnny, for a little over one hundred fifty years after the close of the war, most of the Yankee history books did nothing but tell the world how bad the southern people were and distorted history. Then after that rebellion of 2019 when the government completely took over everything, they practically blotted out that it ever occurred at all. They made it a federal crime for any of the schools to even mention it. So after a couple of generations of brainwashing, the biggest portion of the population didn't even know that it ever occurred. What little information that still existed was in the minds of the old folk still alive and when they tried to tell the younger ones about it, they all scoffed at them and took it for an old fairy tale. After being formally "re-educated", or brainwashed, or whatever you want to call it, people never thought any more of it, 'cause they had never heard of it anyway."

"Don't you think people were smart enough to figure out when they were taking history at school that somewhere down the line there were a few years that were never mentioned?"

"Oh, they were mentioned all right. But people were never really told the truth about what had happened during that time. As far as people were concerned, the 1860's was one of the most peaceful times in American history."

"Well, why would the government want to do that?"

"You see, Johnny, it appears that the government had been lying to everyone for so long about how bad the south was and how good the north was that they were afraid eventually the truth was going to come out and they would have a repeat of what went on back in 1861.

Charles E. Gist

That's what the great rebellion of 2019 was all about. The people just got fed up with the government telling them what to do.

So there it was. Another civil war. And, of course, the government won again. All for basically the same reasons as the first time. They had most of the resources."

"That still doesn't answer my question I asked you a few minutes ago. Why me? Why out of all the people in the world was I picked to be called upon?"

"They sorta left that up to me, Johnny. I kinda done some scouting around looking at different people and you was the one that I chose. I have had a little prior experience at scouting, ya know. Maybe not quite such a wide scale as this. But you know every little bit of experience does help out occasionally. I done quite an extensive background search on you. Well, maybe not so much on you particularly, but on your family in general.

Bet you didn't know that you had no less than forty-two ancestors that fought in the War for Southern Independence. And I am proud to say that not a one of them was on the Union side."

The Other Side of the River

"Forty-two ancestors that fought for Southern Independence. Is that some sort of record or something?"

"Tell ya the truth, Johnny, I don't rightly know. But I can tell ya this: it sure is something that you can be proud of. Let me get back to my story. I'll be dad gummed if you don't ask more questions than either of my two wives ever even thought of asking.

As I was saying, I joined up with the Virginia State Militia."

Johnny said, "Wait a minute. If you were born in Maury County, Tennessee, what were you doing joining the army in Virginia?"

The old man said, "Well, my ma's family was from Virginia and we just happen to be back there a visiting my grandparents when the war broke out. Pa said we had to hurry up and get back to Tennessee so's we could take care of the farm, but I didn't wanna go back. I had heard so many stories about what was going on that I was burning up with war fever when the fighting started. As I was already eighteen years old, Pa said he couldn't stop me from joining up and he was mighty proud to see that I was willing to stand up for what I believed in. He asked me if I would consider going on back to

Charles E. Gist

Tennessee and help out with the farm for a little while and wait and see what Tennessee was gonna decide to do. I told him, 'Pa if I go on back down to Tennessee and wait the war will probably be over and done with. 'Cause everyone knows that one good whipping is all it's gonna take to send those Yanks to running on back where they came from.'

Pa said, 'Yeah, I know your probably right, but just you be careful, son. You'll probably be on home before we get all the cotton picked and the corn put up for the winter anyway.'

So I began my Army career. I commenced to doing all that training of those fancy maneuvers that I was telling you about earlier. Virginia seceded from the Union on the 6th day of May 1861. As a matter of fact, it was on this very day that Tennessee also seceded, so I guess I made the right choice by not going back to Tennessee and wait around to see what they were gonna do. Course, I considered myself almost a veteran by now as I had been in the army for almost a whole month. At that time, we were consolidated into the Confederate Army, COH 3rd Regiment, VA Infantry. But I still hadn't seen the elephant yet. I was sure that it would be just a matter of time and we could take care of that."

The Other Side of the River

"You mean they used elephants to fight in that war?" Johnny asked.

"No, that was just an old army way of saying, 'you ain't seen the elephant until you have experienced combat.' Like I was saying, it wouldn't be long before that situation would be taken care of. I think it was around July 21, 1861 we approached the battlefield at Manassas. It was about 3:00 or 4:00 in the afternoon. We began to see signs of battle to which even us greenhorns could pick up on. There they were as big as day: stragglers going to the rear. I could feel the blood rushing up to my head. I was so mad that I wanted to shoot them myself. How could they disgrace their country by turning their backs on the enemy? Some of them said it was all over and their entire regiments had been cut to pieces. I was proud to see even after these remarks there wasn't a man in our company that fell out of the ranks.

We moved on and after a while we met a general on horseback. He expressed his gratification to our Colonel upon our timely arrival. He gave directions to our Colonel and then rode on off to take care of some other duties.

Charles E. Gist

Apparently, we had been directed to move to our left 'cause that's the direction that we moved in. We were marching in parallel along the rear of the line as you could hear the sounds of the firing in front. The Colonel warned us not to fire as we planned on going to the extreme left of our line before we advanced forward.

As we finally reached the extreme left of our line a messenger approached the Colonel and told him the enemy was giving way and if he hurried, they would soon be in retreat. We had been moving on the double quick for about 3/4 of a mile and were pretty much winded. The Colonel informed the messenger that we would move as quickly as we could get our breath and get organized as we had spread out over a considerable distance at this time.

The messenger dashed off, but returned very shortly and stated that the enemy had only retired his right behind a ridge which was now directly in our front and was moving another column still farther to our right and of us to be on the look our for the other column.

There was a battery of guns a little to the left of our position and it was these guns which had actually started the Yankees to retire. After the woods were completely cleared and we had caught our breath, the

The Other Side of the River

Colonel moved us to the front in order to form a line against the flanking column. I don't mind telling you I don't think I had ever been more nervous before in my entire life. Okay, so I was scared but I was determined that I wasn't going to be counted as one of those stragglers like we had saw earlier, even if I had to die in the process.

Just then, we saw a body of troops move from the woods on our right to another group of trees right in front of us. We could tell those were confederate troops from another regiment. Although I had no idea who they belonged to as there was a considerable amount of smoke from the cannonading of a few minutes before.

Suddenly, there was a rapid fire from the woods to which that other regiment had advanced and a body of the enemy appeared over the crest of a ridge immediately in our front. We quickly formed up in full view of the enemy with their skirmish line about 400 yards in our front as they opened up on us with their long-range rifles.

As we started to advance, the enemy disappeared behind the crest. Another messenger came rapidly approaching and asked the Colonel to not let the men fire on the troops directly in our front, as they were part of that 13th Virginia Regiment. We found out later that this regiment did not actually reach the battlefield at all. The Colonel said, 'But they have been firing on my men.' The messenger said, 'I know they have but it was a mistake.'

The information caused the Colonel to halt the regiment as he rode forward to the crest of the hill to take a look. When he returned I heard him tell the Captain that about 200 yards in the front there was a regiment but as the dress of the volunteers on both sides was very similar and the flag of the regiment was dropping around the flagstaff he would not tell whether the flag was a United States flag or a Confederate flag.

We started to go forward to the crest of the hill; then about that time the cannonading started up again. This caused the regiment in front to start a retreat. This also caused the flag to unfurl and we could plainly see at that time that it was a United States flag. To our surprise, we saw the enemy in full retreat across the plain directly in front of us.

After we had rested briefly, we were ordered to advance in columns of divisions along the same route that the enemy had used and by following the path of haversacks and muskets abandoned, we moved over the battlefield and continued our march to a point just north of a stone bridge.

Nothing could be seen of the enemy and as the Colonel was unfamiliar with the territory, it was impossible to tell which route they had taken. The Colonel decided to stop the pursuit.

So, this was my first battle and I didn't even get to fire one single shot. But it sure was a satisfying sight to see those Yankees skedaddling across that field."

Johnny said, "I bet you sure was scared. I know that I would have been. How did you feel now that you had finally see the elephant?"

"I thought to myself, I knew those ol' Yankees wouldn't stand up and fight. It sure won't be long before it will all be over now. But our sergeant blew that theory pretty fast. 'Don't get so cocky, boys, it ain't over yet. Why you still ain't seen the real elephant yet. You just got a quick glance of his backside as he was trotting on down the road.' That sure took the some of the wind out of our sails."

"They sure had you fooled when you couldn't even tell when there was Yankees standing right in front of you," Johnny remarked.

"Yeah, I know," the old man said. "That's what prompted General Beauregard to design a new flag for the Confederacy. Although it never was officially adopted that was the beginning of the Confederate battle flag."

"What did it look like?" Johnny asked.

"Well, it had a red background and with a blue southern cross which looked kinda like an "x" with a row of white stars forming the cross."

"So that's what kept flashing in my mind since your other visit and dad said it wasn't anything important. Boy, he sure was wrong."

"Don't be so hard on him, Johnny. He don't know any better. That's another one you can blame on the government. Anyway, the south had won a great victory at Manassas against five-to-one odds. With no thanks to me, even though they couldn't say that I wasn't there or didn't attempt to do my part. I couldn't help it if those Yankees high-tailed it outta there before I got a chance to shoot 'em. As it turned out, it would have probably been better if we had lost. We spent the next few months in a false sense of security, with a lot of celebrating and bragging. In the meantime, the north had gotten the message that we were not to be defeated so easily and they started preparing in earnest for war.

It put nearly half a million new men into uniform. It had time to prepare and surround the Confederacy with armies and navies extending from the Atlantic border to the western tributaries of the Mississippi River."

Johnny tried to conceal a yawn.

"It's getting late, Johnny, and you need to get some rest, but don't worry. I'll be back. So you go ahead and get you some sleep."

"Wait a minute! Before you go, I've got one more question for you. In my mind, I've been trying to figure our what to call you. I get tired of thinking of you as the old man. If you don't mind, could I call you Uncle Jim?"

The old man smiled and you could see a twinkle come in his eye. "Johnny, I would be very honored." So Uncle Jim bade him good night and slowly walked away.

The next night Uncle Jim returned and continued his story.

"After the battle of Manassas, we spent the next few months in and around Leesburg, Virginia. We were attached to a brigade composed of three Mississippi regiments and the 8th Virginia, commanded by General Evans. We had in the neighborhood of about 2,000 men.

Charles E. Gist

We had pickets posted and they reported to General Evans the movement of the troops on the opposite side of the Potomac River.

Before daylight on October 20th, 1861, General Evans drew us up in line of battle after listening to a speech. 'Gentlemen, the enemy is approaching by the Dranesville road, sixteen thousand strong, with twenty pieces of artillery. They want to cut off our retreat. Reinforcements can't arrive in time if they were sent. We must fight.' At that time, we were crossed over Goose Creek and spread out along the Dranesville road and waiting for the federal column reportedly headed that way under the command of General McCall.

A few hours after sunrise a federal courier was captured and it was learned that this was just a feint. The main body of the federal troops had crossed Edwards' Ferry which was just above the mouth of Goose Creek and a place called Ball's Bluff where a steep bank hung out over the water.

'If the enemy won't come to us, we must go to them,' I heard General Evans say as we were put into motion and headed for Leesburg. Just as we arrived, the federals that had advanced from Ball's Bluff toward Leesburg held a line of battle supported by four howitzers. The

The Other Side of the River

firing had done got hot and heavy by this time. We didn't have time to get any artillery set up to fire, so General Evans ordered an all out charge. Those terrified Yankees gave way and fled toward the river. It just so happened the direction they were headed was right straight to Ball's Bluff. That was the most scary and sickening sight that I had ever saw in my life. Those Yanks were driven over the edge of the bluff onto the bayonets of their friends 30 feet below. The whole army was retreating, tumbling, and leaping. Hundreds jumped into the rapid moving river. Many were shot while trying to swim away and no telling how many were drowned whether they were wounded or not. Thousands of men ran up and down the banks. Two Massachusetts companies had the sense to surrender under a flag of truce. The shrieks of the wounded and drowning mingled with the shouting of the victorious and the constant rattle of muskets.

I had finally seen the elephant, Johnny, and I sure didn't like the looks of it. But that's the way it was, I went through many more battles after that. I fought for my country because I loved my country and if I had to do it all over again, I wouldn't change a thing, except maybe the final results. Can't nobody tell me that it never happened and I'm not gonna rest until the truth is revealed. It ain't right, Johnny. All that suffering and dying should never be forgotten."

"If I can help it, Uncle Jim, It won't always be that way."

Chapter 2

The War of 2019

"What did the government tell you, Johnny, about the War of 2019?" Uncle Jim asked one night.

Johnny said, "According to the history books, the War of 2019 occurred when a bunch of radical people got together and tried to overthrow the government. So the government had to take over everything to preserve the democratic American way of life. That's when they started all of the social programs to help out everyone to make sure everyone got a proper education and that the people that were able to work had jobs and the ones that weren't were taken care of by the government."

"Well, Johnny, to a certain extent that's true. But I'm sure they gave you a whitewashed version. Back in the early 1990's, there was all kinds of government interference in people's lives and they had a bunch of money-hungry corrupt politicians in Washington and it filtered on down to lower levels of the state and local governments.

People started forming what they called state militias in several different states. They were a kind para-military group that started arming themselves for what they called self-preservation against the federal government. These groups eventually grew into the thousands. These organizations was infiltrated by federal agents and their every movement was reported to the government. The weapons that the militia groups had were varied from shotguns, hunting rifles to the ancient weapons that was used in World War II. They accumulated a large stockpile even though the government had passed laws that the common citizens could not legally possess guns. They felt that they had to for their own protection from the every-growing, powerful federal government.

The headquarters for the National Organization of the State Militias was located in Salt Lake City, Utah.

The leaders of the State Militias called for a big conference on April 9, 2019 in Salt Lake City. They were fed up with being taxed to death. A common person could not be elected to represent the people in Washington. If you weren't rich, you might as well forget it. So they felt it was time to start making plans to overhaul the system and try to get back to the basic things that the principles of this country was founded on. But, of course, like I said earlier, there were spies amongst their ranks and every movement that they made was reported to the federal government.

As much as two weeks prior to the conference, the members of the militias started pouring into Salt Lake City. They started smuggling in weapons for their own protection. They had control of several army tanks and a few jet aircraft, and even a few missiles that they had been able to smuggle into this country. Of course, they couldn't take the larger weapons with them to the conference. They were only able to smuggle in several thousands of rifles and shotguns. They had a good number of stockpiles of ammunition and a fairly adequate food and water supply. So they thought. But the conference numbers kept growing and growing and growing. The leaders were ecstatic at the support that they were receiving.

Finally, the big day arrived. There was approximately two million people gathered there in support of the event. There was all kinds of speeches given discussing the things that the government was doing to the people. Committees were formed to discuss these problems and try to find peaceable solutions. These meetings went on for days. Unknown to them the spies were making routine reports to the government.

Charles E. Gist

The federal government was having meetings of their own. The decision was finally made that the time had come to put an end to what they called the "unlawful attitude of the people" that would be the downfall of America.

Federal troops were secretly made ready for deployment. All military bases were made off limits to civilians except members of the federal government who were given a top security clearance and sworn to secrecy. Military transport planes were loaded with troops and weapons and transported to the outskirts of Salt Lake City.

Upon the completion of the deployment of the troops and army tanks, the attack began. The sky was filled with paratroopers and jets shooting missiles. Any one refusing to go with the military was shot on the spot. In this way, the others were coerced into cooperating.

The people at the conference didn't have a chance. Not with their ancient weapons as compared to the modern weapons of the government forces.

The fighting only lasted for a few days. But the results would last for years to come. Approximately three-quarters of the militia supporters were killed. There was no taking of prisoners. With most of the leaders of the militia movement dead, it would only be a matter of time before the government could completely annihilate the resistance. A few of the militia people tried to make it back to the states where they had come from to rally the people to uprising, but it was to no avail because this had been anticipated. Roadblocks were set up in all directions and patrols were sent out into the surrounding countryside. Several thousand people were captured and executed.

The whole area of Salt Lake City was demolished. The government decided that this was the time to teach the people who was in control. There was a nationwide roundup of known militia members and those suspected of being anti-government. There were mass executions like had never been seen in the world. It made the holocaust of World War II seem like a Saturday afternoon tea party.

Every known library in the United States was taken over by the government and all the history books were ordered destroyed or to be sent to the government to be reprinted, with the government's version.

Everyone's rights as citizens was revoked and they would not be reinstated unless they took an oath of allegiance to the United States government. All the houses were searched for books and weapons, which were confiscated. The penalty for possession of guns or unapproved reading material was death.

So, this was the beginning of the rewriting of American history. The reshaping of America. The beginning of America's great social programs to take care of the American people. This was the War of 2019.

After the war for many years, this was a very desolate country. The will of the people had been broken. Only the rich and powerful people involved with the government or the military faired with any kind of life which resembled decency. The majority of the people were struggling just to survive. After a while, the social programs did improve. The people's lifestyles and things returned to what I suppose they considered as normal, because after a couple of generations they didn't know any better. 'Course it was mostly work, work, work and support the rich government and politicians. Now, I must admit that the government didn't spare any expense when it came to educating the younger generations. Not necessarily in telling them the truth when it came to history. But in teaching them technological skills so they were able to mass-produce products so that America could grow even stronger and richer.

It was several years after the war before the United States started having elections again. The government officials that were in office held those positions until they started dying off. It was passed into law that no government documents were open to the public. They were all considered as top secret and classified for the good of the country and stored in the National Archives Building in Washington, D.C. Only the top officials were allowed access and in this way, the atrocities were concealed.

As you know, Johnny, even to this day there is still no public access to government records. Don't you ever even wonder why?"

Johnny said, "Well, to tell you the truth, before you came along I hadn't really thought a whole lot about it. I'm afraid after having met you that you have probably spoiled my whole outlook on life. I'll probably spend the rest of my life worried about what the government is going to do to us next."

"I didn't come here, Johnny, to try and confuse you or to try and ruin your life. I'm only here to try and tell you the truth, 'cause it's not right that Americans should have to live this way. Not only Americans, but also the whole world should not have to live a lie. I think the time has come. I believe it is your destiny to do something about it. If you think that I am wrong or you can't handle it, I'll leave and you won't ever have to hear from me again."

Johnny said, "No, I don't want you to leave and I know you're right that people shouldn't have to live a lie. It's just that I don't know what to do about it."

"I know, Johnny, but believe me, you'll learn how to take care of it. You're still just a kid and you've still got a lot to learn. Just like everyone else you've been fed a bunch of bull all your life. The only difference is you are the first one that's had the opportunity to learn the truth. I realize that this is a terrible burden to put on your shoulders, but if I didn't feel that you could handle it, you wouldn't have been chosen."

Johnny sadly looked away from the man that he had grown so fond of and said, "I sure do hope that I don't let you down, Uncle Jim."

"So do I, Johnny, so do I. You know all this talking kinda got me to thinking and it reminded me of someone who used to live a long time ago.

The Other Side of the River

There was this feller by the name of Gist who loved the Southland. There didn't nothing make him madder than to hear somebody talking bad about the Confederacy. He even wrote and published a small book of poems about the War of Southern Independence called, "Sworn to Defend" and had it published back in 1995. Never did amount to much. 'Course he didn't get but a hundred copies of it made. Said that was all he could afford. Said that was his contribution to the cause. And he hoped that in some small way that it would help to keep the true memory of the Southland alive after he was gone. He 'bout drove himself crazy trying to prove that he was kin to States Rights Gist who was a Confederate Brigadier General out of South Carolina who got killed while leading a charge on the breastworks at the battle of Franklin, Tennessee back in '64.

He never could make the connection. All he ever found was his great-grandfather who was in the Confederate Cavalry under General Nathan Bedford Forrest. Even at that, all he ever knew about him was what was listed on the muster rolls, Pvt. Calvin Guest, home sick on furlough. So, he didn't ever even find out if his great-grandpa fought or not. But that still didn't stop him from loving the Confederacy or being any

Charles E. Gist

less proud of his private than he would have been of the General.

Anyway, there was this poem that he wrote later after he had published his book and it went something like this.

"Voices"

No more do all the veterans gather
On a single battlefield
To rekindle their old friendships
Or recall those that were killed

So we're no longer blessed with the presence
Of their weathered and furrowed faces
Nor hear their old and shaking voices
Tell of distant times and places

As all their voices are silent now
And no longer do we hear
Of the tales of their heroics
Or the stories of their fear

And the adventures of their lifetimes

>   No longer do they tell
>
>   As some reside in heaven
>
>   And others reside in hell
>
>   But the legacy of the veterans
>
>   Of Southern Independence
>
>   Shall continue to live forever
>
>   Through the voices of their descendents.

Now, Johnny, what got me to thinking about that was that he would probably roll over in his grave if he knew of the War of 2019 and that the voices of the descendents were silenced and that his small contribution to the remembrance of the cause, as he put it, was wasted on deaf ears."

"Are there any of those books still around, Uncle Jim?"

"I don't rightly know for sure, Johnny. They was part of the books that the government gathered up and destroyed. Maybe a few of 'em survived."

"Man, I bet they would sure make some interesting reading."

Charles E. Gist

"Yeah, they would at that, Johnny. You see, I sorta had a sneak look at one of 'em. 'Course, I've kinda done a little more traveling around than you have.

After two long years of fighting, we were battle-hardened veterans. We had killed a whole bunch of Yankees and they had killed a lot of us. One after the other of the friends that I had made in the last couple of years were either wounded or dead. Our force was only about half the size that it was when we had started out. We had long ago about given up on the possibility of the war ever coming to an end.

It was summertime in northern Virginia. It was so hot and dusty as we marched along that you couldn't hardly breathe. A few stragglers would fall out occasionally from heat exhaustion. 'Course that wasn't the only reason. You see food was scarce in these parts by this stage of the war and our uniforms were ragged and plenty of us didn't have any shoes to wear. But we had to keep on moving the best that we could even though we had cuts and bruises on our feet.

Finally, a halt was called and we sat down beside the road to get a short rest under the shade of the trees to get out of the blazing sun. There wasn't much of a breeze blowing so the shade didn't completely cool us

The Other Side of the River

off, but a least it afforded us some protection and rested our sore and weary feet.

I sorta dozed off for a few minutes, I guess, and I got to thinking to myself about my ma back home in Tennessee. I knew she was surely having a rough time of it, since Pa and my older brother had both been killed last year in the fighting down in Tennessee. Anyway, I got to thinking about her and wondering how she was getting by. I mean, here I was up in Virginia and her all the way down there by herself practically and there wasn't anything that I could do to help her.

I had been in the army for two years or more and I hadn't got paid yet. I was a Corporal by now, but a lot of good that did, 'cause I still got the same pay that the privates got -- nothing. I didn't mind so bad for myself, but I sure would've like to have some money that I could send home to help ma out.

As I was saying before, the food was scarce. But the night before while we were camped right out of nowhere, it seems the ugliest cow that I had ever seen in my life just came walking right on up in our camp. That was the unluckiest thing that cow could have done. It was also the last. We had the finest meal that we had eaten in the last several weeks. That was some of the toughest beef that I had ever eaten, but I surely didn't care.

So, I got to thinking about that cow and about my ma and I remembered that it had been a long time since I had prayed to the Lord. I figured it was about time that I did. I commenced to praying to myself.

'Lord, I'd like to take this time to talk to you. I know you're awfully busy, but it won't take too long. So, if you would just take a little time to listen to what I've got to say, it sure would be appreciated.

First of all, I'd like to say thanks for all those fine victuals that you provided for us last night. That was the finest meal that we've had since we started this campaign as foraging is kinda scarce in this part of the country and our supply lines are practically non-existent.

I know, Lord, I don't take the time to talk to you as much as I should and I got to thinking about that. So, here I am, Lord.

What I wanted to talk to you about, Lord, is if you would in you kind way look after our families for us while we're gone and us not being able to provide for them. It's not so much for us, Lord, as it is the loved ones that we left behind. Sure, Lord, it would be

The Other Side of the River

appreciated if you could look after us here in the army, too. But I'm sure there's already plenty of us here that has asked you for that.

Well, that's not all quite true, Lord. While I'm talking to you, I would like to ask you to provide us with the strength and courage to complete the task that we've been asked to do. And if we die in the process, let us put our souls in your hands.

To tell you the truth, Lord, I'm scared. You see, they're using real bullets and canisters out there on that battlefield. Men are dying left and right. Could you see to it to give us the courage to overcome these fears? As I know that our cause is just and we are fighting for what we believe in, which is to protect our homes and families.

Well, I hear our sergeant yelling for us to fall in, so I'll talk to you later and I appreciate you taking the time to listen. In God's name, I pray, amen.

Chapter 3

Johnny's education continued through out his high school years. By this time, Uncle Jim had made him thoroughly familiar with the true facts of what went on during the Civil War.

He listened very intently just to see how gullible the people really were and to see how corrupt the government's version of America's past really was. Of course, he couldn't really blame the people because they didn't know any better. They accepted what they had been told all their lives. Even the instructors actually believed what they were teaching and thought they were teaching the truth.

He never let on that he knew or even suspected that what he was being taught was untruthful. He didn't show any disrespect or rebellion against authority. He was biding his time, waiting for the opportunity to prove to the world and especially America that the government was participating in one of the largest cover-ups ever known to mankind.

If Johnny admitted the truth, he didn't really know for sure how he was going to go about proving it. But nevertheless, he had made up his mind that it was going to be his mission in life to prove just that.

Johnny heard the normal version of military history starting with the Revolutionary War, with the typical war heroes like George Washington, and the Minute Men. He heard all about the French and Indian Wars, the War of 1812, the wars with Mexico, the Spanish American War, World War I, World War II, Vietnam, the Persian Gulf War, and the Rebellion of 2019. But not one word was mentioned about the American Civil War.

As required by law, upon graduation from high school Johnny entered the army. Reluctantly he went through basic training and received the normal brainwashing that all recruits were subjected to. There was only one slight difference. Johnny knew the difference and would not fall victim to the government propaganda.

When Johnny left to go off to the army, he stopped being visited by Uncle Jim. But he was never far from Johnny's mind. One good thing about being in the army was the opportunity to earn money to go to college. He was stationed in Washington, D.C., though for what purpose he really wasn't sure. It didn't make a whole lot of sense to him why he should have to spend week after week on guard duty to make sure that no one had access to the dilapidated-looking government buildings with block walls about twenty feet tall. He wondered what it was that the government was hiding, but he knew better than to ask.

While in Washington, he did run into an old friend of his from way back in junior high school, a young man by the name of Bobby Elmoe. It was nice to see a familiar face for a change. He and Bobby were pretty good friends back then until Bobby's father, who worked for a computer manufacturing company, had gotten transferred to a different district.

Because of his father's influence, Bobby had become quite a computer expert and he was in the intelligence branch of the service.

The two long-time friends stationed far from home decided to go out and get re-acquainted and catch up on old times. Several beers later, it was almost like they had never been separated. Johnny was really glad to see a familiar face for a change. All he had seen lately were sergeants and officers giving orders and blank non-smiling civilians and government workers going about their business on the streets of Washington.

During the course of the afternoon, the two young men got pretty well polluted, okay, so they got downright drunk. Now that was the state of mind they were in when Johnny asked Bobby what he thought it was that the government was hiding behind all those walls that he was assigned to guard.

"Now, you listen here, Johnny Gray, Corporal in this man's United States army. I may be a little drunk, I may be an old friend of yours and it's true that I have access to quite a bit of classified information. But I'm not so drunk that I don't remember some of that old stuff you used to tell me back when we were in junior high school. Those were some fascinating tales that you used to tell me about the War for Southern Independence as you used to call it. I would have thought that you would have given up on that by now. Have you ever thought of writing a book? Anyway, you know good and well that if I did know anything that it would be classified and I couldn't tell you anyway."

"Yeah, I know, Bobby. But I just thought that maybe you might have run across something that might prove that I am right."

"Well, who knows? Maybe one of these days I will. But as it stands right now, I couldn't tell you if I did."

"I know, Bobby. I still say I'm right and one of these days I'm gonna prove it. For now, let's enjoy ourselves while we still have the chance."

So the time passed and the two friends shared stories of what had happened in their lives since they had last seen each other, exchanged addresses and promised to keep in touch. They said their good-byes and went their separate ways.

Johnny continued his ever vigilant and boring duty of guarding the secrets of the government until a few months later when he received word from home that his Uncle George Loomis, his mother's brother, had died. He had accumulated a little leave time, so he was allowed to return to Atlanta for the funeral.

His mother and father met him at the airport, overjoyed at seeing him, but saddened at the circumstances of the meeting.

Johnny's mother began telling a story about her brother. "Now, Uncle George was a pretty wealthy man. That's kinda understandable considering that the biggest interest in his life was making money. Seems like that was all that he ever had been interested in. He was quite a horse trader. Johnny, I remember when George was about 10 or 11 years old, he traded me an old doll that he had picked up somewhere for my bicycle. I thought I had made a good deal because he gave me two dollars to boot and that old bicycle had two flat tires. No one got the best of George, though, when it came to making a deal. He sold that bike to a boy down the street for fifty dollars and two free passes into the movie theater. It seems the boy's father owned the theater and two passes were nothing to him. I still don't know why that boy just didn't get his father to buy him a brand new bike. George did take me to the movie with him, so I guess everything turned out okay."

After the funeral, Johnny was surprised to learn that he had inherited a good sum of money and an old apartment complex from his uncle. George had never married and had no children.

A few days later, Johnny went by to see the apartment building that he had inherited. By appearances, his uncle had spared no expense on the upkeep of the building and it seemed to be in good shape. He learned from the old man who was acting as the manager that it used to be an old government building that George had acquired in one of his deals. Johnny made arrangements for the money from the rent to go into a bank account under his name and for a certain portion to be paid for the management and upkeep of the building.

Johnny returned to the boring routine in Washington to finish out his hitch in the service. He corresponded regularly with his friend Bobby, who had been transferred to a remote location out in Utah.

One day, Johnny got a letter from Bobby and he noticed right off that the postmark was not from Utah, but from Atlanta. Johnny guessed that Bobby had finally saved up enough leave to go home for a while. He also got a letter from his mom, so he thought he'd read that one first. His mother had written the usual greetings and well wishes and at the end of the letter she wrote that Johnny's apartment manager had died. She offered for her and Johnny's dad to take care of it until Johnny could make other arrangements.

These thoughts were going around in his head as he opened the other letter from his friend. He read:

Hello, Johnny!

It's been a while since I've written to you and I bet

you are wondering what I'm doing back in Atlanta. You

know the funniest thing happened while I was in Utah.

I was sitting at my desk, doing my usual secretive thing with my computer, when I heard a noise outside my office. I opened the door to look out and I saw an old man dressed in a gray uniform walking down the hall. I yelled at him to stop, but he just turned and walked away. I figured I had better let someone know he was there, so I turned around and went back into the office. When I shut the door, the water cooler that was next to the door fell off and landed right on my foot. To make a long story short, it crushed the bones in my foot and after reconstructive surgery, the army discharged me. Can you believe that? I still don't know who that old man was and everyone else said they hadn't seen anyone who wasn't supposed to be there.

Anyway, here I am back in Atlanta trying to piece

together my life. I've been thinking about trying to

find someplace to start a computer software business.

But I haven't had any luck as yet. Just thought I'd

let you know what has been going on. Take care and

stay in touch.

Bobby

Johnny immediately sat down to write to his friend. He told Bobby he was sorry to hear about his accident and that he was lucky to be out of the army. He wrote that by coincidence he had a solution for both of their problems if Bobby was willing to work for him. Bobby could take over managing the apartment complex and have a place to live and could also set up shop and start his computer business if he wanted to. Johnny asked him to go by and see his mother and make the necessary arrangements and he would sign the papers to get Bobby a salary started from the rent proceeds.

So began the partnership and the continuation of a lifelong friendship. Johnny couldn't help but think, "So Uncle Jim is up to his old tricks again. I don't suppose he had a plan when he pushed over that water cooler, did he?"

Johnny's time was finally over and he was discharged from the army. He returned to Atlanta for a little freedom and relaxation before he decided where he wanted to go to college.

As for Bobby, he was doing just fine in his computer business and was only walking with a slight limp. He was glad to see Johnny come home and threw a big party to celebrate his friend's return. When the party was over, the two friends sat around talking and the conversation turned to the accident with Bobby's foot. Johnny said he thought it was fate that had caused it.

"Yeah," Bobby said. "It sure was. If it hadn't have happened, I'd still be in Utah or some other Godforsaken place instead of here with my best friend and I wouldn't have the computer business which I've always wanted for as long as I can remember."

"I don't know, Bobby, but I've got a feeling that there is more to it than what meets the eye. I think it happened for a reason."

"Yeah, I know. My getting my foot broke and booted out of the army is gonna help you prove that great theory of yours."

"Well, we're just going to have to wait and see. But mark my words. One of these days, I'm gonna prove it. I've got a feeling that you are going to play a part in it."

"Sure, sure. We're both gonna of down in history as the boys who rediscovered America." Bobby closed his eyes and passed out from the effects of the alcohol he had drunk.

Johnny covered him with a blanket and stumbled off to his own bed. He could hardly stay awake himself.

Chapter 4

Johnny's first few days at college weren't too bad. Even though he must admit that it was a little confusing. Everything would be all right as soon as he learned his way around. If he could handle four years in the military, surely he could handle himself at school. After all, that was the reason he went ahead and stayed the extra two years to get his college tuition paid in full.

He figured he had an advantage over most of the students since he had a couple years of maturity on them plus the discipline that he had been used to.

Johnny wholeheartedly applied himself into the lifestyle of the modern day educational facility. Determined to get the most of of the opportunity to further his education. He took the required courses of Advanced Trigonometry and Geometry, English, Computer Science, and American Government Philosophy. He also signed up for American History, as this is what he planned on being his major.

It wasn't too long until he fell into the normal routine of going to classes then back to the dorm or the library to study for exams, which were almost a daily occurrence in one class or another. And of course as could be expected, his favorite subject was history. He finally did conquer the finer points of trigonometry and geometry, but it wasn't without a struggle. He couldn't quite get it to sink in as to what good it was ever going to do him in his chosen field. He sure didn't want to be a rocket scientist or physicist. It was too boring to suit him. He'd take good old people-related subjects anyday.

He would get occasional breaks and go home to visit his parents and his friend, Bobby. Bobby was growing extremely wealthy with his computer business. He had landed a few government contracts.

Johnny still hadn't had any visits from Uncle Jim in the past few years but he still hadn't forgotten the things that the old man had taught him nor had Johnny given up on the task of proving to the world that the war for Southern Independence had occurred. He just wasn't quite sure how he was going to do it.

Toward the end of the fourth year of college, Johnny was in his Advanced American History class, which was taught by an elderly gentleman named Professor Albert Livingston. They had arrived upon the point in time of the 1860's, and true to style, he heard the same story about how prosperous and peaceful that the United States was. When he could finally stand it no longer, he asked the kindly professor, "Professor Livingston, what can you tell us about the War for Southern Independence?"

The professor paused before he answered. He gave Johnny a surprised look as he said, "Mr. Gray, I'm afraid that I must refrain from making too much comment on that subject, as it is common knowledge to everyone who is old enough to think, the War for Southern Independence never occurred. And furthermore, it is a subject that is not to be discussed in the classroom according to law."

You could hear the giggles and the murmurs from the other students in the classroom.

"Now, we shall continue with our lesson for today."

As the class was ending and the students started to file out of the room, Professor Livingston said, "Mr. Gray, could I please have a word with you?"

Johnny replied, "Sure, Professor."

After everyone had left, the professor asked Johnny to take a seat. "Mr. Gray, I must say that I'm worried about you. You are a brilliant student, but that comment that you made during class. Surely, you must know that to some people it is almost heresy to bring up such a subject."

"I know that, Professor. But I've stood it as long as I can and I had to see what your reaction would be. I know that you seem to be an honest and sincere person and I personally believe that the government is involved in a gigantic cover-up to hide the true history of America. There. I've said it. That's what I've been wanting to say for years."

The professor sat silently for a few seconds rubbing his hand on his forehead, as if he had a headache. Then he raised his head and looked at Johnny. "Mr. Gray, let me make my point very clear. This job is not just what I do for a living. It is my life. I love history, but to tell the truth, I have been suspicious of the government's version of everything for years. I have always believed the whole story wasn't coming out. But I have no choice. Without evidence to prove otherwise, I must teach history as I am told to teach history. Do I make myself clear, Mr. Gray?"

Johnny grinned and said, "Sure, Professor. But I intend to prove it one day. When I do, will you be willing to change your teaching philosophy?"

The Other Side of the River

"Certainly, I will Johnny, but in the meantime, would you please refrain from referring to that particular subject while in my classroom?"

"No problem, Professor. No problem."

So, Johnny completed his college education. He received his degree to be a professor of history after completing a year of internship as an assistant professor. But for now, it was time to go home to Atlanta for a while and relax and unwind. He moved into one of his apartments in the building that he had inherited from his uncle. Bobby, of course, just had to throw another one of his famous parties and along with that came a night with no sleep and a day of recovery.

Johnny spent several days getting reacquainted with the old neighborhood and visited with people he hadn't had a chance to spend much time with in the last eight years. A few of the older people had died off, some of the younger ones had moved away, and some were off in the army. There were even a few new people around that Johnny had never met before. It didn't take long for Johnny to get to know most of these people as they had all heard about him anyway. It seems that his parents were quite proud of their son and they never hesitated to tell anyone they met about their son who was going to be a professor of history one day.

Bobby was sitting in his living room late one night working on a computer program for one of his clients when the light went out on the desk lamp. "Come on, give me a break," he muttered to himself as he got up and went into the next room to get another light bulb. He returned and screwed in the bulb and flipped the switch off and on. Nothing happened. "Must be a tripped circuit breaker," he thought to himself. "Well, if I'm going to get this program finished tonight, I guess I had better go down to the basement and check it out. He retrieved a flashlight and a screwdriver from one of the drawers in his desk and headed down the hallway to the door leading to the basement below. He opened the door and shined the light around on the landing until he spotted the light switch. He flipped it on and the basement was partially flooded with light. Bobby proceeded down the stairway to the far wall, which was nearly covered with breaker panels. He had to use his flashlight in the part of the basement that held the panels because the light bulb there was burnt out too. He shined the light over the panels looking for the number of his own apartment." Ahh there it is number

1B." Bobby opened up the door on the panel box and shined the beam of light onto the circuit breakers and sure enough there was a red window indicating that the breaker was tripped. Bobby reached out with his right hand and reset the breaker. As he did so his hand slipped off of the edge of the panel box which was located on the far right of the row of panels. When his hand slipped he struck the red brick wall with the blade of the screwdriver which he was holding in that hand. A large chunk of bricks fell out of the wall and the screwdriver made a metallic sound echo into the stillness of the room. "Well so much for your uncle's fine upkeep Johnny my boy," thought Bobby.

Bobby turned and started to walk away and then he thought," now wait a minute what was that metal that I hit with the screwdriver? "Probably just some old water pipes." Bobby turned back around and shined the light into the opening and peered in. "Hmmm, looks like a metal door or something. I can see the cracks of the seams along the edge. I wonder what's hiding back there? I'm not gonna bust this wall down to find out. I better tell Johnny about this."

Bobby went back up the stairs until he came to apartment 1A, which Johnny occupied. He knocked on the door.

"Yeah, who is it?"

"It's me, Bobby."

"Come on in, Bobby, the door's open."

Bobby went in and told Johnny about what had just happened in the basement.

"Well, I guess we had better go down and see what it's going to take to fix it," Johnny said.

The two friends went down to the basement to examine the brick wall. As Johnny shined the light into the opening, he could clearly see the edge of a doorway.

"Bobby, go get us a hammer and a pry bar, and let's see what's on the other side of this doorway."

Bobby returned with the tools and they started removing the bricks. In a few minutes, they could clearly see the whole door in front of them.

"Well, here goes nothing," Johnny said as he turned the key which was in the doorknob. The door creaked as they stood back and peered into the darkness.

"Hand me that light, Bobby."

Bobby handed Johnny the light. Johnny shined the light into the pitch blackness and they could make out a stairway descending down into the further reaches of the dark.

"Are we sure we want to go in there?" Bobby asked.

"Don't tell me you're afraid of the dark, Bobby?"

"No, I was just wondering if maybe it might be dangerous or something."

"Well, there's only one way to find out," said Johnny as he stepped onto the stairway.

Bobby hesitated then reluctantly followed. Farther and farther down they went. They could smell the musty air, which had a slight sweet smell to it. As they reached the bottom of the steps and shined the light around, they saw row after row of books on shelves.

"So this explains that sweet smell. It's the old leather covers on all these books. What sort of place is this? There's more book in here than they have at the university," Johnny said.

"I don't know, but it's gotta be old. There's no telling how long that wall has been sealed up," said Bobby.

Johnny reached up and pulled the first book that he came to off of the shelf. With a trembling hand, he laid it down on a table and wiped away the dust that had accumulated. He took a seat in a rickety old chair because his legs were too weak to stand and his heart was beating so fast he could hear it pounding inside his head.

Cautiously, he opened the cover and read the first page: The Roster of Confederate Soldiers 1861-1865. Volume I A - Rk to Bell, GWR M 253-1-M253-30. A Multi-Volume Set edited by Janet B. Hewett, Broadfoot Publishing Company, Wilmington, NC, 1995.

Johnny turned the page and started to read the introduction.

"The Southern men and boys who answered war's klaxon in 1861, and their neighbors and kinfolk who entered service later in the war under various promptings, marshaled into units and armies that are among the most famous in all of recorded military history. Until now, however, no comprehensive listing of the Confederacy's fighting men has ever been published..."

Johnny glanced down the page and continued to read not realizing that he was reading out loud in a very uncontrolled voice.

"It remained for Tom Broadfoot to get the job done as a private venture more than three quarters of a century later. My God, Bobby! Do you realize what we have here?"

The Other Side of the River

Bobby was leaning on the table as white as if he had just seen a ghost and was unable to speak for a few seconds. "Yes, it means that this is probably the evidence to prove that you have been right all these years I've had to listen to your cockamamie stories about the War for Southern Independence. And it also means that if we get caught with these books, we'll probably get shot or spend the rest of our lives in prison. What now, Johnny? What are we going to do now?"

"I don't know, Bobby. I'm confused. I need time to think. But one thing I know for sure is that we've made a big discovery here and we've got to keep it to ourselves for a while until we can look this stuff over and figure out exactly what it is we have. Come on, let's get on outta here for now and take a little while for this to sink in so we can think straight."

So they started heading toward the stairway exit. But as they did, the beam from the flashlight passed over a sign that was leaning against the edge of a bookcase. The sign read, "National Archives, Atlanta Branch."

The two men stood looking at other in the dim light produced by the flashlight.

"Come on, Bobby. Let's get on outta here for now. We'll be back later. We got some thinking to do."

They went up the stairway to the level of the upper basement.

"We want to make sure we keep this door locked at all times, Bobby," said Johnny as they reached the level of the building where the breaker panels were located. He closed the door behind him and twisted the door handle to make sure that it was locked.

They went to Johnny's apartment and sat down at the table before he realized that he still had the book in his hand. He gingerly laid it down on the table and stared at it as if he was in a stupor. He gently took his fingers and rubbed over the surface, which used to be smooth but now he could feel the cracks that time had produced upon the hard surface of the cover.

"How about some coffee, Bobby?"

"Uh, well, sure." replied Bobby.

Johnny got up and turned on the coffeepot.

In a few minutes, the aroma of coffee filled the room and Johnny got up and poured two cups. As he sat back down and took a couple of sips, he finally spoke.

"I don't know about this, but I think maybe what we have found here is repository or something of the

The Other Side of the River

federal government. The sign said National Archives, Atlanta Branch. We're going to have to go back down there and look at some of the other books to really figure out for sure what's going on. But as far as I'm concerned, this is conclusive evidence that I've found to substantiate my claim that the War for Southern Independence occurred. And I'd be willing to bet anything that there is more where that came from."

Bobby just sat there with a blank look on his face as if he was in shock.

"Come on, Bobby, snap out of it. What are you thinking?"

"I'm just thinking about the firing squad."

Johnny laughed for the first time. "Don't be so pessimistic. My friend, this is the find of the century. Stick with me and I'll make you famous!"

"Yeah, or dead," Bobby said sarcastically.

"Come on, Bobby, flop down there on the couch and we'll talk about it some more in the morning."

After a few hours of restless tossing and turning, Johnny awoke to the smell of bacon cooking, the smell of coffee and the sound of dishes banging from the kitchen. He slowly got up and headed toward the sound. Bobby was just finishing setting the table for breakfast.

"Good morning, Johnny. How did you sleep?"

"Lousy," Johnny replied. "How about you?"

"Man, I slept like a baby once I got over the firing-squad jitters. And have you figured out the great mystery yet?"

"I believe I have, but you're probably not going to believe some of it."

"After what I saw last night, I'll probably believe just about anything.""

After getting down a few sips of coffee and a few bites to eat, Johnny began to perk up a little.

"Okay, Bobby, here's the scoop. The way I've got it figured. Someone about halfway told me about this a long time ago. Don't ask me who because I'm not ready to divulge my source. It appears to me, I have been correct all along when I said the War for Southern Independence occurred. But you see, after the Rebellion of 2019, the government confiscated all the evidence they could find that there had been such a war. What they couldn't confiscate or hide, they destroyed. Apparently, there was a repository for information, a study center or whatever you want to call it, in Washington D.C. for information on the history and people of the United States. That was the main

The Other Side of the River

headquarters. But there must have been branches of the repository that had copies of the same records that were kept in D.C. The very building that I now own must have been one of those branches. Who knows how many more of these places exist? Or if they exist at all anymore. I think when the government started destroying all these records, someone had sense enough to hide some of them down in the basement and blocked off the entrance before the thugs that were in control arrived. Maybe they saw it coming quite a bit in advance. But anyway, luckily they succeeded in doing what they had set out to do and that was to preserve what little of the history of the United States that they could. I don't know who it was, but I think we should be very grateful."

"You mean to tell me that all our lives and all the lives of the people living since 2019 have been a lie?" Bobby asked.

"That's exactly what I mean. But to find out just how much of a lie, I think we have got to go back down in the basement."

"Well, what are we going to do about it, Johnny? You know that if we try to go public with this information that we could be in serious trouble."

"I know, Bobby, but I don't think we have much choice. We can't just ignore it. Before we go back down there, give me some more time. There's one person I need to go see for advice."

"Okay, Johnny. I sure do hope that we are doing the right thing. I still keep getting visions of the firing squad."

Chapter 5

Johnny rapped lightly on the door and an old lady opened it up and said, "Yes, may I help you?"

"Yes, ma'am, you must be Mrs. Livingston. My name is Johnny Gray. I'm a former student of the professor's. May I speak with him?"

"Why, yes, of course. Johnny Gray, why I've heard so much about you. Albert is really very fond of you. Please come in. I'll tell Albert that you are here. He will be delighted."

As Johnny stepped inside the doorway, the professor came out of the adjoining room to see who his wife was talking to. When he saw Johnny, a big smile spread across his face and he sped up his steps to cross the room with his hand extended.

"Johnny Gray! What a pleasant surprise to see you. Please, come in and make yourself comfortable." He turned to his wife. "Martha, this is the young man I have been telling you about."

"I know, Albert, he introduced himself at the door."

"And Johnny, this is my wife Martha."

"It's a pleasure, ma'am." Johnny said as he nodded.

"And what brings you all this way, Johnny, my boy?" asked the professor.

"This, Professor Livingston," Johnny said as he handed him the package that he was holding in his hands.

The professor reached out and took the package and laid it on his knees as he reached into his shirt pocket and pulled out his glasses and placed them on his face.

He unwrapped the package and sat there staring at the book and absentmindedly ran his fingers over the small cracks on the cover. He slowly opened up the book and read the title and the color drained from his face. "My God, Johnny! Where did you get this?"

"I thought you might be interested." Johnny could hardly keep from grinning.

"But, but these ... these books are not supposed to exist," the professor stammered.

"Yeah, I know," Johnny said, "and the War for Southern Independence never occurred either."

Johnny explained to the professor how he had acquired the book and the professor sat and listened. Slowly, the color returned to his face. As Johnny finished, the professor said, "Well, this is very interesting. You see, this is not the first book that I've seen like this. When I was a little boy, my father had a whole set of these books. He showed them to me one time. And only once. He told me that I should never tell anyone about them as it was against the law to have them. It wasn't long after that our house caught on fire. Everything we had was destroyed. All these years, I have kept that promise that I made to my father. But under the circumstances, I have no choice but to confide these secrets to you."

"I kinda suspected that day in class, Professor, that you knew more than what you were letting on. So, what I came here for was to see if you might be interested in going back into that room with me and my friend, Bobby Elmoe."

"Johnny, I'm an old man, but I wouldn't pass up an opportunity like this for thirty years to be added to my life. Let me get my things together and we shall leave right away."

The professor, Bobby and Johnny descended the stairway leading into the basement; each loaded down with various items that they deemed necessary to perform the task at hand.

The equipment mainly consisted of extension cords and lights. They also carried with them a video camera with which they intended to record their discovery. They had also carefully checked to make sure that no one was around to see them before they entered into the basement.

After plugging in the cords and stretching them down the final stairway, they hung the lights around the room. Then, they hooked up the video camera to one of the electrical cords so as to conserve the battery. Previous to this, the professor had been operating the camera. "We must record all of this activity, it must be documented to prove that this is not just a hoax. Our very lives may depend on it." the professor said.

"I wish you wouldn't say that, professor. It brings back images of the firing squad again. I expect the goon squad to show up at any minute and cart us away." Bobby said.

Johnny said, "I think we're ready to start looking, professor, if you are."

"Certainly, Johnny, I can hardly contain myself any longer."

The three men started taking books off of the shelves and examining them, reading various titles as they wiped away the dust that had accumulated for so many years. There were so many titles and subjects that they could not begin to keep up with them all. There were county

The Other Side of the River

histories, state histories of every state, biographies of well-known people and a lot of people that the trio had never heard of. There were indexes to census reports from 1790 to 2010.

"Now, this is interesting," the professor said. "I never knew that the government kept records of the census. This should prove to be very revealing indeed."

"And, would you look at this, professor, volume after volume of books on the Civil War."

"How in the world did the government ever manage to conceal all of this from everyone?"

"The government is a mighty powerful and rich force, Johnny, and if you have enough power, enough money and enough time, you can manipulate people to believe just about anything." said the professor.

Stamped inside the front cover of all the books were the words: Property of the National Archives, Washington, D.C.

"At least your theory was correct about there being a National Archives in Washington, Johnny." said Bobby.

Johnny looked up from the book that he was studying and said, "Yeah, there's no doubt about that and I'll just about guarantee you that at least one of those locations with all the block walls around it I spent years guarding is it, too." He held the book open to show the title and stamped page to the video camera.

"Would you look at this, boys?" said the professor. "We have what appears to be card catalog files to rolls of microfilm on every subject in the world. But I don't see any microfilm."

"I don't think I've ever seen any microfilm," Johnny said.

"Johnny, they quit using that method of storing data years ago, once the computer age came along. It's no wonder you've never seen any. But I still don't see any rolls of microfilm. Perhaps whoever stored this stuff down here didn't have time to save all the records before they had to seal this place up."

"I think you're probably right in that assumption, professor. The government probably either confiscated or destroyed them. It could be possible that they were transferred to Washington. We'll probably never have the opportunity to find out for sure. We can't just go to Washington and say, 'Oh, excuse me, would you mind if I have a look at your rolls of microfilm that I know you keep concealed behind those block walls with all the little guards around them.'"

That brought a light chuckle out of the other two men.

"Listen to this, professor," said Johnny as he started to read from a stack of old newspapers that were piled on a table in the corner of the room. "I met Mable Hamilton at the Latter Day Saints Church Genealogical Library last week and entered a whole new world of exploration. It's addicting, like putting a puzzle together, but frustrating...' Then it goes on to say, "Since 1930, the church has sent crews throughout the world to film genealogical records. These are all stored in a granite vault in the Wasatch Mountains outside of Salt Lake City. These records are in an earthquake-proof and climate-controlled environment.

One copy of each record is also in the Church Genealogical Library in Salt Lake City, and multiple copies have been duplicated for individual churches to rent or buy. All materials are available either on microfilm, microfiche, or CD rom disks for computer.

In addition to the voluminous files, which the local church maintains, further materials can be ordered from the Index put out by the head library in Salt Lake City. They have been cataloged under localities or states, author, title and subject matter (such as records,

Indians, etc.). The library also contains a copy of the International Genealogical Index containing 250 million names, most of them Mormon Church members, with an addendum of 40 million names recently added. There are 10,000 names on each microfiche broken down into states and counties.

On computer, there is an ancestral file database with 200 million names. Nonchurch members are invited to submit genealogical charts, pedigree sheets, and descendancy charts for inclusion in the files. It is even possible to download files to your own 3.25 disk, which will run on the Personal Ancestral file computer program or other genealogical programs. You may also secure hard copies on a printer.'"

Bobby said, "Hey, maybe we ought to make a trip out to Salt Lake City and check out this place. Maybe they've got more records there than we've got here."

The professor and Johnny exchanged glances.

"The only thing wrong with that suggestion, Bobby, is if you'll remember, the history that was taught in high school, you'll recall that Salt Lake City was the location of the Rebellion of 2019. It was supposedly totally destroyed."

The Other Side of the River

"Yeah, I remember that vaguely, but what about that granite vault that was mentioned in the article? It was supposed to be earthquake-proof and climate-controlled. Maybe it was also bomb-proof or maybe they just forgot about it and besides, it's possible there maybe a lot more records there in a lot better shape than what we have here. Can we afford not to try and find out?"

Johnny and professor gave each other another look and both nodded in agreement.

"I'm afraid you're right, Bobby. We can't afford not to go and see if anything still exists out there."

Chapter 6

The three friends spent the next few days preparing for their nearly two thousand mile journey to Salt Lake City. They used the excuse that they were going on a vacation camping trip as they went about the task of gathering up supplies. Finally, they had everything that they thought they would need for the trip loaded into the four-wheel drive vehicle Johnny was able to obtain at a decent price through a distant cousin who ran a used car dealership. He said that it was about time he owned his own transportation anyway; he was getting tired of riding the commuter train everywhere he went. He vaguely wondered to himself why they still called it a truck. It more closely resembled the old time space shuttles without wings.

They studied several maps and decided on the best route that they needed to take to reach their destination. As he was pouring over one of the maps, Johnny said, "Wait a minute! I just thought of something. If you'll remember the article that we read in that newspaper, it said the vault was located in the Wasatch Mountains outside of Salt Lake City."

"Yes, that is true to my best recollection."

"Then, look here, professor, on this old map. It shows the Wasatch Mountains a little to the east of Salt Lake City near a place called Heber City."

"Then perhaps we won't have to go all the way to Salt Lake City. That's just as well if the stories are true that nothing was left there anyway."

"That was my thought, exactly, professor."

Bobby returned from running an errand and asked what they were talking about. Johnny and the professor explained what they had been discussing and showed him the map. As Bobby looked over the map he said, "Johnny, you remember when I was in the army I was stationed in Utah."

"Sure, I remember."

"Well, look at this old map. Right next to Salt Lake City is Fort Douglas Military Reservation. That's where I was stationed! I never realized that it was that close to Salt Lake City. We flew in there and were not allowed to leave the base. When I left, we flew out so I never got a chance to find out where in Utah that we were actually located. All I ever heard it called was Fort Douglas. It may be a good thing that we don't have to go all the way to Salt Lake City, because we don't want anyone who is tied in with the government questioning why we are out there. If the government doesn't know where that vault is or even if it exists anymore. How much chance do you think that we'll have of locating it"

"Well, I calculate the odds at about 50/50," said the professor. "Either we find it or we don't, but I believe it exists. We all know that we must try. If we don't find it, then we will just have to go with the evidence that we have already accumulated to convince the people that they have been deceived. But the more evidence we have, especially from different sources, the more apt we are to succeed."

"Bravo, professor!" said Bobby.

"Then I suppose we are ready to hit the road?" Johnny asked.

"I've been ready my young friend, I've been ready." the professor replied.

As expected, the trip going out west was pretty much uneventful. They had hour after hour of pleasant driving and plenty of time to discuss the possibilities of what they might find.

On the morning of the fifth day after leaving Atlanta, they arrived at the small town of Heber City, Utah. They stopped at a local cafe to eat breakfast.

Johnny explained to the waitress that they were on vacation and were looking for a good spot to go camping.

"Oh, if you're looking for a good spot to camp and fish, you need to go up to the Jordanville Reservoir."

"How do you get there from here?" Johnny asked.

"Take Highway 189 north out past Wasatch Mountain until you come to Highway 150. Go east about five miles and the reservoir will be on your left-hand side of the road. They have some of the best cabins and the most beautiful view you'll ever see in the world." the waitress replied.

"Well, I sure do thank you, ma'am, for the information. You wouldn't be interested in going camping would you?"

The girl blushed and said, "No, I better stay here, but I sure do hope you guys have a good time."

After the girl left, Bobby asked, "What would you have done if she had said yes, Johnny?"

Johnny grinned. "I guess she'd have just gone camping with us."

After breakfast, they loaded back in the vehicle and headed north out of town in the direction of the Jordanville Reservoir. A few miles out of town, toward the east it was possible to see that one mountain was a little higher than the rest.

Johnny said, "I think that's probably Wasatch Mountain. Keep your eyes open, Bobby, and let's see if we can find a side road headed in that direction.

About a mile farther down the road, they came upon a dirt road headed back in an easterly direction and gradually it started to turn a little to the north. After traveling about three miles on this road, they came to a big clearing and the road ended.

"Looks like this is the end of the road, boys. Let's take a look around and see what this place looks like. A few hundred feet off in the distance they could see where the ground started to elevate at the base of the mountain. They got out of the vehicle and could hear the sound of running water. They decided to check out the source of the sound. As they went around a gigantic boulder right at the base of the mountain, they came upon the remains of what used to be a large building. It looked as if it had burned years ago. Coming down off the side of the mountain was a small waterfall, which formed a pool at the bottom. They could see the reflection of the sunlight on the water and through the mist they could make out a beautiful rainbow.

"This has got to be it!" exclaimed Johnny. "We're going to find the pot of gold at the end of the rainbow."

"I don't know about that, Johnny, but there's no denying that it is beautiful," said Bobby.

"Professor, why don't you take a little look around here and we'll set up camp?"

The professor nodded his head as he stared in awe at the waterfall and the rainbow.

Bobby and Johnny unloaded the conveyance and set up the tent while the professor looked around. As they were setting up the table and stools, the professor walked back up from where he had been looking at the remains of the building. In his hand, he was toting a piece of rusty, partially burned out rectangular metal about three foot long and about a foot wide.

"Now, this is interesting," said the professor and he held the object out for the boys to examine. They could just make out the word "asylum" along one end of the sign.

"Now, that's what I call a vacation," said Bobby. "How many people do we know that would travel 2,000 miles just to spend a little time relaxing at a crazy house?"

"Crazy house? I don't see a crazy house, do you professor?" asked Johnny.

"No, not yet, but by the time we get through, we'll probably be lucky if they even consider putting us in a crazy house rather than shooting us."

The three friends had a good laugh at this comment.

Suddenly, Bobby realized something. "Hey, wait a minute! We've got to get some pictures of this."

He ran over to the truck and retrieved the camera.

"Here, professor. Hold up the sign. Johnny, stand beside him."

The two men did as instructed and Bobby took several snapshots of them and their surrounding location. After he was through, he set up the video camera and filmed for a few minutes. He sat the video camera on the tripod and turned it off.

"Did you get plenty of shots, Bobby?"

"Got some great shots," he replied. "We may need these as evidence when the goon squad shows up. Or if nothing else, we can show how we spent our vacation."

It was getting pretty late in the day when Johnny made the comment; "We had better look around and find some firewood. It gets pretty cold in these mountainous regions. We can build a fire in this area right over here. Looks like someone else had one here before."

"Wonder who camped here before?" Bobby asked aloud looking at the small circle of rocks where someone else had built a fire.

"No telling," Johnny replied. "I'm sure there's plenty of local people who know about this place."

They each went off in different directions and in a few minutes, they had a large pile of wood neatly stacked next to the tent.

"I don't know 'bout y'all, but all this work has made me hungry," Bobby said.

"You're always hungry," joked Johnny.

"Well, I'm a growing boy!"

"I don't know about the boy part, but you sure are growing!" Johnny jibed.

"Ha ha!" Bobby replied. "I'll go ahead and get the fire started and get us some supper going."

"Okay, Bobby, I'll get us some water from the pond. Could you look in that box, professor and see if you can find the coffee?"

"Sure, Johnny, a good cup of coffee sounds mighty fine right about now."

When Johnny returned with the pot full of water, Bobby had the campfire ready and was opening up a large can of beef stew and poured in into a pan. He placed it next to the campfire as he waited for the flames to burn down a little. The professor was up to his elbows in flour as he rolled out dough to make biscuits. In a few minutes, the reflector oven was placed next to the campfire to reflect the heat on the pan containing the biscuits.

"I didn't know you knew how to make biscuits, professor," Johnny commented.

"Are you kidding? Look at this protrusion!" the professor laughed as he patted his stomach. "I haven't always been a college professor, you know. Some of my fondest memories are of my father and I camping together."

With the biscuits browned, the stew steaming and the coffee boiling, the three friends sat down around the campfire to enjoy their meal as they continued their conversation. Off in the distance, they heard the voice of a man attempting to sing his own version of "Sweet Betsey from Pike." He was humming loudly and when he didn't know the words, he would shout the words, "Sweet Betsey from Pike!"

"What in the world is that?!" all three seemed to ask as they looked at each other. From around the large boulder came an old man leading a mule loaded with a backpack. A pick and shovel protruded from the ropes wrapped around the pack. He looked like an old prospector straight out of the old western days.

He stopped singing as soon as he saw the strangers and stood there looking at them. Suddenly, a big smile spread across his grizzled face. He turned and looked at the mule and said, "Well, Nellie! Looks like we got company!"

He walked over to the three men and tied the reins to a tree branch.

"Y'all fellers work for the government?" he asked.

"No sir, we're just on vacation," Johnny replied.

"Good, I don't cotton much to government people. Name's Lige Nedpelter, some people say I'm crazy. That coffee sure does smell good."

"Well, have a seat and help yourself," said Johnny as he reached into the box beside him and pulled out a cup. "There's plenty of stew and biscuits here, too, if you're hungry."

"Much obliged!" the old timer said.

"My name's Johnny Gray, these are my friends Bobby Elmoe and Professor Albert Livingston. We're on vacation from Atlanta, Georgia."

"Well, if you come all the way out here just for a vacation, then I must not be the only one around here that's crazy!"

Bobby nodded his head as the professor extended his hand and said, "It's a pleasure to make your acquaintance, Mr. Nedpelter."

"Just call me Lige. Don't like my last name. Ain't much I can do about it, but it still don't make me like it."

They sat in silence for a few minutes as they finished up their meal and laid their dishes to the side.

Lige took a deep breath as he wiped his mouth on his shirtsleeve. "Mighty fine meal. As I was saying, some folks say I'm crazy. Could be maybe they're right. Don't matter much one way or the other, anyway."

"What brings you out this way, Lige?" Johnny asked.

"I live out here. Can't afford no vacation. Not just here. All over the place. Been prospecting for gold. Ain't found the motherlode yet, but one of these day's me and Nellie, we are gonna strike it rich.

The Other Side of the River

That's Nellie right over there." He pointed toward the mule and she brayed as if she knew that he was talking about her.

"This here's one of my regular spots. Don't many folks come around here 'cuz they think it's haunted."

"Why would they think that?" asked Bobby.

"Don't rightly know myself," said Lige. "Guess 'cuz they used to be an insane asylum right here on this very spot. That was many years ago, though. The government burned it down during the last rebellion. Lots of the local people claim there's ghosts around here. But they don't bother me and I don't bother them. Maybe ghosts don't mess with crazy people. Or maybe crazy people ain't got sense enough to be scared of 'em. Got any sugar?"

"Sure," said Johnny and he handed him a bag.

Lige took it and poured a big handful and walked over to feed it to Nellie. "Nellie loves that stuff, never eat it myself. Anything that tastes that good has got to be bad for ya. Probably kill ya. I ain't ready to go yet. Still gotta find that motherlode."

"Whatever got you to wandering around out here looking for gold?" asked the professor.

"Got tired of the government interfering with everything. Couldn't even go to the bathroom hardly without the government wanting to know about it. Tax this; tax that, it's unlawful for you to do this or that. Told you when I walked up here, I didn't care for the government. Never have and never will. Out here, at least so far, they ain't messing with me and Nellie. Probably will, though, if we ever find that motherlode. That's if I tell 'em. Just as soon spend the rest of my days doing just what I'm doing right now. Living free. Or just as near to freedom as anyone can expect to obtain in this country anymore."

"Do you mind if I take your picture?" Bobby asked.

"Well, I don't know. I haven't had a picture in years."

"It would make a good momento of our vacation scrapbook," said Bobby.

"Well, if you just gotta have one, ya gotta take one of Nellie, too. I wouldn't want her to go and get jealous on me." Lige went over and untied Nellie from the branch and stood holding the reins in one hand and his old slouch hat in the other.

The Other Side of the River

Bobby affixed the flash attachment to the camera and asked Johnny and the professor to get into the picture with Lige and Nellie.

Johnny said, "Bobby, why don't you set the timer on the camera, put it top of that rock there and get in the picture with us?"

"Okay, Johnny," Bobby answered. He made the necessary adjustments and slid in beside the others. The camera snapped and the flash went off. Nellie brayed and tried to get away from the bright flash. Lige put his hand over her eyes and whispered into her ear as he stroked her on the neck and she soon settled down.

"We've had 'bout as much excitement as we can stand for one night, so I guess we better mosey on," said Lige. "I 'ppreciate the supper, it was mighty fine."

"Why don't you go ahead and spend the night here with us, Lige?" said Johnny. "We've got plenty of room and plenty of firewood, something to eat and you are sure welcome to stay."

"Naw, boys, me and Nellie, we gotta get going. We still gotta a lot of looking to do if we ever gonna find that motherlode. If'n you boys ever make it back out this way, stop on in. I'll be around these parts somewhere and maybe we'll run into each other again." He shook each one of their hands, took Nellie by the reins, and walked off into the darkness singing his own rendition of "Ol' Brown Rosie, the Rose of Alabamie". When the sound of his voice faded away, only the sounds of a whippoorwill and a coyote were heard.

"That Lige sure is a strange character," commented Bobby.

"I don't know that he hasn't got more sense than all of us," said the professor. "Given, it is strange for someone in this time and age to be wondering around alone searching for treasure. But at least he has his freedom."

"What's so strange about it, professor? Aren't we searching for a treasure of our own?" Johnny asked.

"That's true, Johnny, but whatever we find, I'm sure we won't be able to keep it a secret from the government. Nor do I think we want to, when the proper moment arrives."

"I can hardly wait for that moment to arrive, professor," said Johnny.

"I can't wait, either. I can almost hear the orders being given now. 'Ready, aim, fire!'" added Bobby.

The Other Side of the River

"Don't be so pessimistic, Bobby. Maybe they won't go through all the formalities." Johnny teased as he cleaned up the dishes from supper.

"Now, that's a comforting thought," said Bobby sarcastically. Johnny and the professor chuckled at the look on Bobby's face.

The trio spent the next several days exploring. They searched through the ashes of the burned out building and the surrounding area and didn't find anything of significance. They were about ready to give up and came to the conclusion that they were searching in the wrong area. Early one morning after spending a restless night, Johnny was unusually quiet as they were eating breakfast. He seemed lost in his own thoughts.

"What seems to be troubling you, Johnny my boy?" asked the professor. "You aren't giving up on us are you?"

"No, I'm not giving up, professor. I guess I 'm just a little frustrated that we haven't found anything. I know we're close. Real close. I guess I expected that it wouldn't be so hard to find. That we'd just walk right out here in the middle of these mountains right to that vault we are looking for."

"If it was that easy, Johnny, it wouldn't have stayed hidden as long as it has."

"I know, professor, but it seems that I've been looking all my life. I'm just tired and I didn't sleep very well last night. I kept tossing and turning and had these thoughts going around in my mind. It was all jumbled up and I can't remember all of it. But somehow, it involved that old prospector that we met the other day. I know it sounds a little strange, but I remember him reciting a little verse to me."

"And what did Lige have to say, Johnny?" asked the professor.

"He said, 'Go to the mountain formerly used for the insane. Ascend to the top to reach the right plane. Look to the west for the proper degree. Totally concealed by a giant of a tree. There you will find the treasure that you seek. Long ago abandoned on the lonely mountain peak.'"

After a few moments of silence, the professor spoke. "We cannot ignore your dream, Johnny. Perhaps in some strange way, that's the answer to the question."

"I don't know, professor, but I guess we'd better go have a look."

The Other Side of the River

By midmorning, they had reached the top of the mountain. They decided to take a breather while sitting on top of one of the many rock formations which protruded from the mountainside among the trees. They drank water from their canteens and lay their heads on their backpacks as they rested and gazed off in a southerly direction over the treetops. Far off in the distance, they could just barely discern the outlines of the town of Heber City.

"Look at that view, professor! You can't tell me this is not one of the most beautiful places in the world."

"I wouldn't even attempt to, Johnny," replied the professor as he reveled in the beauty of the countryside. "It's just a shame that we've lived in a state of deceit for so long."

"Maybe it won't always be that way. After all, this is a great country. Like that Yankee President said in one of those books we found, 'You can fool some of the people all the time but you can't fool all the people all the time.'"

"Yes, but they've been getting away with it for a long time now," said the professor.

"Well, that's why we're here. To prove otherwise and I intend to prove it if I have to die in the process."

"Let's hope it doesn't come to that, Johnny."

"Maybe it won't, but we'll never find out sitting here on our backsides. Guess we'd better move around a little. But first things first. I'll be back in a minute, nature calls."

Johnny stepped around the left side of the rock formation out of view of his companions to relieve himself of the two cups of coffee he had consumed with his breakfast. Before turning around, he gazed off to the west. He could see a giant tree that stood out from the rest.

"Professor! Bobby! Come here quick!"

The two men came running to Johnny's side.

"Look at that tree over there. Remember what Lige said in my dream about a giant tree off to the west."

The three men quickly started working their way in that direction and soon came to the base of a tree, which was about thirty feet in diameter.

"This looks like a Sequoia," said the professor. "They don't usually grow this far east. The only place I've ever heard of them growing is in California."

The Other Side of the River

"I don't know what kind of tree it is, but look how much larger it is compared to the others," said Johnny.

Bobby backed off about a hundred feet and took some snapshots of Johnny and the professor standing at the base of the tree.

As they were looking around, Bobby pointed to what appeared to be hoof prints in the soft earth on one side of the tree. Without speaking a word, the trio followed the prints around the back of the tree almost to a bluff on the mountain. There were several small trees and underbrush between the giant tree and the mountainside and they had to part them with their hands to push their way through. Once through this growth blocking their way, they saw the entrance to a cave. They stopped in their tracks and stood looking at each other. Johnny could feel his heart racing in his chest and he knew that he wasn't the only one that was having the same sensation.

Johnny stepped into the entrance of the cavern and into the total darkness. He felt in front of him along the edge of the wall and stopped as his two friends bumped into him from the rear.

"We're gonna have to have some light in here," Johnny said in a shaky voice. "Let's go back outside and get our flashlights out of our backpacks."

They felt their way back to the entrance and emerged into the bright sunlight and squinted their eyes to readjust them after being in the total darkness.

After arming themselves with their lights, they started to go back in when Johnny said, "You know, we might not find anything in there. It may just be an empty cave and it could be dangerous. We better take a rope and tie to one of these small trees and feed it off behind us in case we get turned around in there. And we've got to be careful that we don't step off into some bottomless pit."

With that, they each looked into their backpacks and retrieved a rope.

"To be on the safe side, why don't we tie the ropes around our waists and go in one at a time and when the one that is leading runs out of rope, the next one attaches to that one and follows? If it's alright with you guys, I'll go first."

"Suits me, Johnny," Bobby replied. "It's your dream."

The Other Side of the River

The professor nodded his head in agreement as he was tying one end of his rope to a small tree and the other end around this waist.

After hooking the ropes around each other and checking for strength, Johnny said, "Well, here goes nothing. If I find anything or reach the end of my rope, I'll give three sharp pulls and y'all can proceed to follow. Bring extra rope with you."

Johnny entered into the total darkness of the cave for a second time. As he entered, he turned on his flashlight and shined it around reflecting the little crystal particles off the cold granite walls. Cautiously, Johnny proceeded, watching very carefully where he stepped and hearing nothing but the echo of his own footsteps, his own breathing, and feeling the vibrations in his chest as his heart seemed to be working overtime. After several minutes which seemed like hours, Johnny entered into what seemed to be a wider portion of the cave as his light would not penetrate into the darkness far enough for him to clearly discern one wall from the other. Johnny felt the rope tighten around his waist and thought to himself, "Must be the end of my rope." He gave the rope three quick successive jerks and felt the same in return. Then the rope went slack. "Guess Bobby must be coming on in."

As he shined the light around, he noticed what looked like some kind of cabinets over to his right and he started to walk in that direction. Just at that moment, Bobby caught up with him.

"Found anything yet?" Bobby asked.

"There's something over here. I haven't had a chance to look at it yet."

The two walked over to the area where Johnny was shining his light so they could get a better view.

"What is it?" asked Johnny.

"If I'm not mistaken, it's an IBM model 1204 computer. These things haven't been manufactured in well over 50 or 60 years."

Upon closer examination, Bobby made a discovery as he shined his light over the surface of the computer.

"I made a mistake, Johnny. It's not a model 1204, it's a model 1205," Bobby said as he ran his fingers over the letters printed on the side of the cabinet. "But that still makes it over 50 years old. There's one other thing, too, Johnny. If there is a computer down here, they had to have had an electrical source to run them." Bobby was shining his light around until he found what he was looking for. "There. See that conduit running up the wall? Let's trace it back and see where it was fed from. They were in the process of tracing the conduit when the professor arrived.

"Whatcha got boys?"

"We found an old set of ancient computers, professor, and we're trying to trace its source of power. If it's still operable, we may be able to get some light in here," said Bobby.

"Now this is exciting!" exclaimed the professor.

"Over here, Bobby," shouted Johnny as he focused the beam from his flashlight on several electrical panels that were mounted on the wall. "Bobby, you're the closest thing we've got to an electrical expert. So, I guess it's up to you to figure out what to do."

Bobby shined his light around for a few seconds before he said, "This looks like the main breaker to me. I'll turn it on and see what happens."

As Bobby turned the breaker on the room was flooded with light from several locations.

They stood in awe as they surveyed the large open area within which they were standing. Opposite each other were rows of desks with computer consoles sitting on top, each with a chair neatly pushed up against each desk. There were several tables sitting around with chairs and some sort of screens with little reels with handles on them.

"And what are these?" Johnny asked.

"Those, my friend, are microfilm readers," Bobby replied. "One of the old storage methods for records was putting the information on microfilm and using these machines to read the information the film contained."

They opened one of several doors and peered inside and saw row after row of batteries.

"Looks like they probably used a solar collector to keep these batteries charged to operate the lights and equipment. That way, they could keep the location of this place secret by not having power lines ran in here. Pretty ingenious if I have to say so myself."

The three moved further into the cave and came to a large room filled with shelf after shelf of books pertaining to genealogy and government records from all over the United States and the world. The professor slowly walked from shelf to shelf reading the titles of the books as he rubbed his fingers over the spines as if he was a blind man reading in Braille.

The professor was totally immersed in his own little world. Johnny and Bobby proceeded into the next chamber which was even larger than the last. It was filled almost to capacity with cabinets containing microfilm and computer discs neatly arranged in alphabetical order according to subject names and years which came to an abrupt halt in the year 2019.

"Looks like we found what we came looking for, Bobby. But now that we have, what are we gonna do about it? We can't take it all with us and we can't reveal it's location."

"You are right up to a certain point, Johnny. But you'd be surprised at the amount that we can take with us. By interlinking those old computers to my computer, I should be able to make copies of these records that are on disc into the memory bank of my computer. The modern computer has almost an unlimited capacity as compared to these early versions."

"I knew I wanted you to come along for some reason. Bobby, now I know why!"

"Ha, ha!" said Bobby. "And all this time I thought you just kept me around because you liked me."

They spent the next few hours looking around at the discoveries that they had made. Every once in a while, one would call out to the others to come over and see what they had found. After a few minutes discussion, they headed off on their own again.

"My friends, this is all very interesting," said the professor. "But I'm an old man and I tire easily. Perhaps we should head back down the mountain and pursue this adventure tomorrow. I think I've had about all the excitement that I can stand for one day. Besides, I'm getting hungry."

"I'll vote for that, professor," said Johnny.

"Me, too!" exclaimed Bobby. "In the morning, we can start downloading some of this information into my computer to take back to Atlanta with us."

The three friends did not sleep very well that night after the excitement of the day. After tossing for several hours, and numerous conversations, exhaustion finally prevailed.

The following morning, they slept later than usual, which was just as well because a blanket of fog converged into the area and prevented them from being able to return to their explorations. They spent the extra time discussing what they had already seen and gathered up the equipment they needed to take back into the cave. They needed more tape for the video camera, several boxes of CDs for Bobby's computer, and the various cables that he said he would need to hook up to the ancient computers to be able to download the information. Finally, the fog lifted and they started their ascent up the mountain. As they reached the entrance to the cave, Johnny stopped suddenly and looked around as he pointed to the ground.

"Look here. There's more of these same hoof prints we saw yesterday and they're on top of our footprints. I hate to tell you this, gentlemen, but we are not alone here."

"Who do you think it might be?" asked Bobby in a shaky voice.

"I don't know. But my first guess would be that it might be Lige and Nellie. Maybe he's looking around in there for that motherlode he kept talking about."

"Yeah, but if that's so, why were there hoof prints going into the cave yesterday? Why didn't we see him if he was in there?"

"I don't know," Johnny replied. "Maybe he was further back inside."

"Look, boys!" said the professor pointing a little over to one side. "Here's another set of prints going back in again. I don't claim to be a tracker, but perhaps Lige and Nellie only come out after dark and then go back in before daylight. If that's who it is."

Bobby felt a cold chill go up his spine and shook uncontrollably for a second the way they say you do when someone walks over your grave. "I don't like the looks of this, Johnny. Not one little bit," said Bobby.

"Don't take it so hard, Bobby. Lige seemed harmless enough. We're probably just letting our imaginations run away with us." Johnny reassured him.

"Yeah, and I suppose we're imagining these hoof prints, too. Next thing you'll be telling me is that Lige and Nellie didn't drop in and see us the other night," said Bobby.

"Well, what do you want to do about it, Bobby? Just load up and hightail it back to Atlanta?" asked Johnny with a wounded look on his face.

"Deep down that sounds like a pretty good idea to me, but I know we can't, so we may as well go on in and retrieve the information we came to get. We would look pretty silly going back empty-handed," said Bobby as he mustered up his courage and entered the cave for the second day in a row.

They spent the next several days getting up early and going to the cave and making copies of all the records

The Other Side of the River

that they could find and taking unusual books back down to their campsite to be loaded into the truck. Each afternoon as they left the cave, they would take a branch and erase their footprints at the entrance of the cave. Each morning when they returned, there was a new set of hoof prints going in each direction. Though not wholly comfortable with the situation, the trio continued upon the task they had started.

While looking through a tall stack of books back in the far depths of the cave, the professor made another discovery. He noticed more of the strange hoof prints and a set of men's footprints that they had not seen before. Not being the hero type, the professor decided to go and get the other two men before he proceeded any further. Upon their return to the area, they followed the prints to a previously undiscovered door. Slowly, Johnny reached out and opened the door. He shined his flashlight into the darkness. He could just make out the shape of a small table and what appeared to be a cot over next to the far wall in the large room. As they entered into the room, they could also see that one corner contained what looked like a small pile of old dried out hay. Upon closer examination of the haystack, they found a pile of bones that looked like it belonged to a small horse or possibly a mule. They moved further into the room and approached the cot. Lying on it was a human skeleton holding a pencil in its right hand. The left hand was resting up on a closed book, which lay upon the white glistening rib cage partially covered by the remnants of the cloth shirt or jacket he had been wearing at the time of his demise.

Johnny reached over toward the body and retrieved the book from beneath the skeletal fingers. His arm and hand, blocking the beam of light, created a giant shadow. Just as he touched the book to remove it, the skull rolled to one side and the mouth closed as if it was finally relaxing after all these years.

"This should explain a few things," Johnny said as he opened up the cover to the first page and read aloud. "Lige Nedpelter, May 13, 2019."

"Don't you think we have accomplished what we came here to do?" Bobby asked in a weak voice as he nervously looked in one direction and then another as if he was expecting something to suddenly appear out of the darkness. "I believe we have, Bobby," said Johnny as he stuck the book into his coat pocket. "It should be interesting to see what Mr. Nedpelter has to say."

"We can look it over when we get back to camp."

The Other Side of the River

As they reached the entrance to the cave, they noticed that the only footsteps that were visible were heading inside. They slowly descended the mountainside to their camp. Each were lost in their own thoughts and they tried not to notice as each one took an occasional glance back over their shoulders as if to see if they were being followed. Not a word was spoken between them until they had reached the campsite and they saw that the sugar container had been tipped over, spilling the contents on the ground. A few white granules were embedded in the hoof prints next to their tent.

Johnny opened up the book as he sat next to the campfire that evening. "My friends, I think the time has come for a little bedtime story." Johnny methodically turned the pages of the diary and read, "'It was Saturday, April 9, 2019. Shortly after 9:00 a.m., I heard the jet airplanes fly overhead as they headed into Salt Lake City to drop their payload of destruction. A few seconds later, I heard the sound of machine gun fire and bombs exploding. Great clouds of black smoke and fire could be seen rising off in a westerly direction from my home. Luckily, I lived in the suburbs, which were not on the initial target list for the first wave of attack. Having never been married, I lived alone. I lived close enough to work that I could walk, therefore I had no private transportation. I could see that the ground attack was heading in my direction, so I hurriedly gathered up a few belongings along with my canteen, rifle, and camping utensils stored in my barn. I had my mule, Nellie, which I used occasionally when I went prospecting to relax and get away from my job record keeping at the Genealogical Library in Salt Lake City. I had an idea what was going on. This was later confirmed by broadcasts on the portable radio I carried with me. All you could hear was the government propaganda of how they had defeated the rebel forces that were planning the overthrow of the federal government. My first thought was to find a place to hide. I went east with the intention of trying to reach the cover just north of Heber City. It took me several days to reach my destination. I had to spend a lot of time hiding from the patrols of army troops that were scouring the area between Salt Lake and Heber City. When I arrived, I found the smoldering remains of what used to be an insane asylum at the foot of Wasatch Mountain. Luckily, the entrance to this depository is concealed and the location is not well known. I could tell from the radio broadcasts that the government was on a witch-hunt and out to destroy anyone or anything they thought had anything to do with the so-called rebellion. I knew if they ever found me, I was a goner because everyone in town knew how I felt about the government. My only hope for survival was to stay hid out until this crisis blew over.

I have spent several weeks holed up here in this place, and I have seen an occasional patrol of troops passing close to this area on the few times that I have gone out to get water from the pond at the bottom of the mountain. The food is running low and I have started to ration the amount of food that I eat daily.'"

There were several more pages telling of more close encounters with army patrols and about the propaganda that was broadcast over the radio before the batteries went dead and Lige lost contact with the outside world.

Toward the end of the book, the writing was getting worse and Johnny could hardly make out the words Lige tried to scribble. Lige was getting weaker every day…

"'Only hope that someone finds this one day, someone who is decent and honest and not a puppet of this godforsaken government.'"

Johnny closed the book and stared into the fire. He wouldn't look at the others. He hoped they couldn't see the tears that rolled down his cheeks.

The next morning, they loaded up their truck and headed back to Atlanta.

The trio spent the remainder of the summer studying the information they had accumulated. By the time September and the beginning of the college fall semester arrived, the professor and Johnny were fairly familiar with the history of the Civil War and were totally aghast at the way the federal government had covered up and deceived the American people.

Bobby, in the meantime, had created computer programs and stored all the information on discs. He made several copies of the discs and stored them in different locations. If the authorities seized one copy, there would still be a backup. If they were arrested or executed by the government, maybe somewhere in the future, someone would discover them and know what had gone on.

Johnny and the professor paced nervously across the front of the classroom as the students started pouring

The Other Side of the River

in. After everyone had taken seats, the professor stepped up to the podium.

"Good morning. My name is Professor Albert Livingston and this is my colleague, Mr. Johnny Gray. We will be your instructors for this semester in American History. I would like to take this opportunity to welcome each and every one of you to this class. I hope that we can have an enjoyable time. Now, Mr. Gray here, has a few things that he would like to say."

"Thank you, professor." Johnny said as he took his place at the podium. "As the professor said, my name is Johnny Gray, and I, too, would like to welcome all of you. I think each and every one of you sitting in this classroom will be able to leave this class as a better person, secure in the fact that you will be better informed than you have ever been in your entire lives. You may be more confused, but I guarantee that you will definitely be better informed. You see, we plan on teaching history as it really happened. You will not only be learning history, but you will be a part of history. This very day, this very moment is a milestone in American history. I would like to be the first to tell you that you have been lied to and you have been cheated. It is the right of every American to be informed and to have a proper education."

Johnny looked around the room. Every eye was focused on him and he seemed to have their full attention, as the usual whisperers were not carrying on any conversations. "Perhaps our methods are unconventional, but the time has arrived for a change. The time has arrived for the truth. The normal politically correct history that you have been taught all your lives will no longer be valid in this classroom. I'm not referring to all that you have been told because sometimes even liars stumble on the truth. I am referring to a particular time in our history. The years are 1861 - 1865. I am sure that by trying to tell you the truth that there will be dire consequences. But I have no choice. You have been misinformed. Not intentionally by the ones who taught you, because they did not know any better. They had also been misinformed.

Let me tell you a little story. It's one that the professor doesn't even know about. I know you'll probably think that I'm crazy when I tell it to you. Do you like ghost stories?"

Several students nodded their heads yes.

The Other Side of the River

"Well, good because I'm gonna tell you one. It's not just an ordinary ghost story. It's a true ghost story. I'm sure you're wondering what a ghost story has to do with history. In this case, plenty, because it was a ghost that started the pursuit of the truth."

It was quiet enough to hear a pin drop. Even the professor seemed to be all ears as he looked intently at Johnny.

"I'm sure all of you are familiar with the Great Rebellion of 2019, which occurred in Salt Lake City. That's no lie; it happened. But ever since that time when the government took over everything, the history of America has been distorted. Let me get back to my story. There was a twelve year old boy who kept having dreams about an old man who kept coming into his room at night and telling him strange stories about things that the boy had never heard about before. Or at least, for a long time the boy assumed that they were dreams. When this boy tried to discuss this matter with his father, he was told that it was probably something that he had eaten that disagreed with him that was causing the boy to have strange dreams. Well, the boy couldn't stop eating, so he kept having these dreams..."

Johnny went on to describe to the students the clothes the old man was wearing.

"Is there anyone here that knows what kind of uniform the old man had on?"

Several students shook their heads.

"I didn't think anyone would, so I'll tell you what kind of uniform it was. It was the uniform of a sergeant in the Confederate States army."

The students looked puzzled.

Finally, one girl asked, "Mr. Gray, what is the Confederate States army?"

"I thought you'd never ask" Johnny replied. "The Confederate States army is the army of the Confederate States of America, which was in existence during the years of 1861-1865. And does anyone in this room other than the professor have any idea as to where the Confederate States were located at?"

Again, there were "no" responses. Johnny went on to name off all of the states that were in the Confederacy.

One of the students sitting toward the back of the room raised his hand as he spoke. "Mr. Gray, why is it that we have never been told of the existence of this Confederate States of America and why is it that they no longer exist?"

The Other Side of the River

"Like I told you before, the government has distorted the history of America to make it appear that the Confederate States of America never existed."

Another student raised his hand and Johnny pointed to him. "What about the old man in the story you made up. Why was it necessary for the Confederate States of America to have an army in the first place?"

"It was necessary for the old man to have on an army uniform because he was in the army during the time of the War for Southern Independence."

"Mr. Gray," said a young man in the front row. "Why would these southern states want to secede from the Union and why would the government want to cover it up? And why should we believe you when everything you are telling us is contrary to everything we have always been told?"

"There were many reasons why the southern states united together into a southern Confederacy. The main one was northern aggression of southern rights. The politicians in Washington were passing laws that hurt the southern economy, such as tariffs on the exportation of cotton, which was the mainstay of the southern economy at that time. The south was mostly an agricultural society compared to the industrial society in the northern states. Part of the cotton industry work was performed by slave labor. There were people in the north called abolitionists that wanted to abolish slave labor. Most of the slaves that were in the south were imported into this country through northern parts and sold for millions of dollars to the southern plantation owners. Although, slavery was one of the reasons for the war, it was not the main reason until it was pushed into the limelight by abolitionists. They tried to make it appear that the reason the north was fighting was to free the black people from slavery and the southern people were fighting to keep them in bondage. Personally, I don't buy that theory. There were only one in fifteen people in the southern states that owned slaves. These were mostly the aristocratic rich plantation owners. So why should the other ninety-four percent of the people fight just to give the rich people the right to own slaves? Abraham Lincoln, who was the president of the United States, issued an emancipation proclamation almost two years after the war began. The emancipation proclamation freed only the slaves in the territories that had seceded from the Union. It didn't mention anything about freeing any of the slaves still being held in the northern states. The south considered themselves as a sovereign nation. Therefore, the northern president was over-exceeding his authority. If he was so concerned about slavery, why did he not mention the slaves in the north? This was all a political ploy to stop England and other countries from recognizing the Confederacy as an independent country and to prevent them from giving aid to the Confederacy. The constitution of the United States at the time plainly gave each state the right to secede from the control of the federal government if they were not satisfied with the way they were being treated. The textbooks used in the United States Military Academy at West Point were also stressing this same point. Yet, when the southern states tried to exercise their constitutional right of secession to create their own democratic government, the northern states refused to allow this to happen peaceably. You asked why the government would want to cover all this up. The answer is simple. Prior to the Great Rebellion of 2019, it wasn't covered up. It wasn't always truthful as most of the history books were written from the northern point of view. They were the victors as far as they were concerned. But even as long as one hundred years later, many southern people felt that the war still wasn't over. Maybe the pitched battles had ceased, but some of the issues were still not settled. This was what led up to the Rebellion of 2019. Just plain government interference. The Confederacy still lived in the hearts of many thousands of descendants of the lost cause, as some people called it. Many people belonged to the heritage organizations whose members were proud that their ancestors had the courage to stand up and fight for what they thought was right. There were several flags representing the Confederacy. But the most controversial was the one known as the battle flag."

Johnny reached beneath the podium and retrieved a two-foot by three-foot poster that he had drawn to show the students what the battle flag had looked like.

"This flag was created by Confederate General Pierre Gustav Toutant Beauregard after the battle of first Manassas, or Bull Run as some called it. The flags used by both sides were similar and were hard to distinguish from each other in battle with all the smoke in the air, especially when there was no breeze and the flags were hanging down the side of the flagstaffs. What made this flag controversial was the fact that it was also used by what was termed 'hate groups.' Groups such as the Ku Klux Klan who believed in white supremacy. Therefore, it was considered racist by some people. The black people especially considered it as a symbol of slavery. To the true historical heritage organizations, it was not considered racist, but as a symbol of heritage. Depending on their point of view, people either loved it or hated it. Someone was always protesting the Confederate battle flag. Most of the time, the government would support the people that wanted to get rid of it. They didn't want to offend anyone. That became known as 'being politically correct.' I personally do not believe in slavery. But the south was not the only guilty party in the slavery issue. The northern slave traders made millions of dollars by selling the slaves to the south and then turned around and said that the south had to set all the slaves free without any compensation. How can anyone blame these people for being angry at losing millions of dollars?

Anyway, at the time of the Rebellion of 2019, the government decided that this was the time to put the issue to rest once and for all by quelling the rebellion and destroying the history books and rewriting history to omit the existence of the War for Southern Independence."

Charles E. Gist

"That was a very amusing story, Mr. Gray," said a boy in the back of the room. "Maybe you should consider writing fiction stories as a profession rather than being a history teacher."

Johnny smiled and answered, "Perhaps that is an idea, but it is not my intention. Every word that I have told you is the absolute truth and Professor Livingston can vouch for my integrity. We do have evidence to substantiate all the facts that I have just conveyed to you. This should prove to be a most interesting semester in American History. I invite each and everyone of you to continue to attend my class if you are interested in learning the real history and not the politically correct hogwash that we have all been fed for the last three or four generations in America. Our time has run out for today. I look forward to seeing all of you again tomorrow."

The silence no longer prevailed as the students started talking among themselves as they filed out of the room. Some couldn't quite figure out if this new professor was some sort of wacko with a good line of bull or really sincere in what he had said. If he was correct in what he had said, then he was also right in saying that this really is a momentous turning point in the history of America. Most of the students were not really sure one way or the other, but they could hardly wait until tomorrow to hear what Mr. Gray would say then.

"How does it feel, Johnny, to finally get this thing unloaded off your shoulders?" the professor asked after the room had cleared.

"It feels good, professor. Real good. Though I must admit that it is a little scary."

"Let me tell you, son, I hope we haven't stepped in over our heads. But there's no turning back now. Even if none of those people believed a word you said, before the day is over it will be all over campus. They couldn't keep something like this quiet even if their lives depended on it."

"Or ours," said Johnny with a sheepish grin.

"Do you want to take bets on how long it will be before we hear from Mr. Farnsworth?" asked the professor as he made reference to the president of the college.

"Sure," Johnny said. "A week if we're lucky. Tomorrow if we're not."

After lunch, Johnny repeated his performance to the afternoon class of students with pretty much the same response. He ignored the remarks that came from the back of the room as one of the students got up and left.

After the class was over, Johnny told the professor, "Well, so much for being lucky. I think I just saw it all walk out of the room, probably headed straight for Mr. Farnsworth."

"Well, we both knew that it would just be a matter of time. Perhaps it's better to go ahead and get it over with."

"I know, but I would at least like to show them some of the evidence that we have before they shut us completely down."

"Tomorrow, Johnny, tomorrow," said the professor as he gathered up his briefcase and patted Johnny on the shoulder. "Come on, let's go. I want you and Bobby to come over to my house for supper tonight. It may be the last chance that any of us get to have a decent meal. The goon squad may be showing up sooner than we expected."

Johnny, the professor, Bobby, and the professor's wife, Martha, were in the middle of eating their supper when Martha asked her husband, "Albert, how did it go today? You didn't have any problems did you?"

"No, of course not. It was just a typical, normal day other than the fact that we have slightly changed the curriculum. As a matter of fact, I was very proud of the way Johnny conducted himself and rather pleased at the response of the students. It's almost like a large percentage of the students weren't really surprised. But of course, there were a few that didn't cater too much to the notion that their past education was irrelevant."

"But I'm worried, Albert," said Martha. "About what the consequences of all this is going to be."

"Oh, don't you worry your pretty little head, Martha." The professor reached out and patted his wife's hand. "A price must always be paid for progress."

"I know, but it still doesn't stop me from worrying. I just don't know what I'd do if you weren't around."

"Well, I don't think the fireworks will really start until after Bobby brings in those video tapes and shows them to the class. I think those videos should convince even some of the skeptics. You do still want to go through with this, don't you Bobby?"

"Oh, yes sir, professor. I may be a coward at heart but I wouldn't want to miss this. Maybe I can come in disguised s a Confederate soldier, show them real quick, and escape out the back door."

"None of 'em has ever seen what a Confederate soldier looks like, so maybe you might get away with it. But just in case, you better keep on running when you get outside," joked Johnny, as he slapped his friend on the back.

After the meal was over, they spent an hour or so visiting before they decided to call it a night. As Johnny and Bobby started to leave, they failed to notice the two men who were lurking in the shadow of the building across the street. Neither one noticed the vehicle which fell into the line of traffic behind them as they headed for home.

"FPF 219 to headquarters, we have the two suspects insight, headed north on McHenry Avenue."

"Ten four." Came the reply. Then there was silence.

Johnny and Bobby arrived back at their apartments. Both were dead tired, so they went straight to bed. Johnny had just barely gotten to sleep when a sudden shaking of the bed woke him up.

"Hey, sleepyhead! You gonna sleep your life away?"

"Uncle Jim!" exclaimed Johnny. "It's been a while. Where in the world have you been?"

"Oh, I've been around. Been pretty busy, though. Don't know if I'm cut out to be holding all those conferences with Marse Robert and Jeff Davis. Somehow, it just don't seem like I fit. But ya gotta do what ya gotta do."

"Oh, come on, Uncle Jim. We both know you're as good as they are, and I'm sure they think so too or else they wouldn't have picked you to do the job they wanted done."

"Well, maybe, but I sure do think they could've carried a lot more clout to the importance of this mission than what I have. I just dropped in to see how ya been doing and to tell you I seen a couple men snooping around in here earlier. They were searching around over there in those desk drawers."

Johnny got up and walked over to his desk. He could see where the drawer had been broken into. He opened it up and looked inside, felt way toward the back of the middle drawer. "I see they found what they were looking for. I had a copy of some of the computer discs in here that Bobby had made on some of the information that we found in Utah. Luckily, we have other copies."

"Guess the cat's outta the bag," said Uncle Jim. "Had to happen sooner or later."

"Yeah, but I sure would've liked for it to have been later. I haven't even broken the ice good with my classes. I wanted to get some more details out to them so they wouldn't think I had gone completely crazy. We were gonna start showing them some videotapes and some of the information on the computer discs tomorrow. That's what it's gonna take to convince these people that we're not making all this up."

"Well, you said you had some more copies of it. So why don't you go a head and use them?"

"Oh, we will. I just don't know how fast they are gonna move on this. They may not give us time to. I'm sure they'll want to keep it as quiet as possible."

"Which reminds me, I better go warn Bobby so he can get another one of the copies that he's got stashed."

"Yeah, well, I gotta be moving along myself. No rest for the weary. Just wanted to stop in and say 'hello' and to let you know I hadn't forgot about ya. You keep up the good work and watch your back."

After Uncle Jim had left, Johnny went down the hall and knocked on Bobby's door. Bobby came to the door and opened it while rubbing the sleep from his eyes. Johnny explained to Bobby that two men had been in his apartment and had found the copies of the discs, which he had stored there.

"Okay, I'll drag out some more for tomorrow," said Bobby in a sleepy voice.

After Johnny returned to his apartment, Bobby lay back down across his bed. After a couple of minutes, Bobby jerked back up quickly, suddenly wide awake. "Why hadn't I thought of this before?" he thought as he went over and flipped on the switch to his computer. In a few minutes, he was through with his task and he stumbled on back to bed. He slept like a baby until the sound of the alarm clock woke him up the next morning.

Bobby and Johnny informed the professor of the events of the previous evening just as soon as he arrived to the classroom.

"I can't say that I'm really surprised," said the professor. "You know how the government works. If they are going to control people, they have to keep on top of things. I told you yesterday that we couldn't keep this under wraps very long. It was probably that one boy who left out of here yesterday like his coattail was on fire. Probably went straight to Mr. Farnsworth. Guess I'd better go call Martha and let her know I may be late for dinner tonight."

In a few minutes, the professor returned.

"How did she take it?" asked Johnny.

"She was crying, but she said she'd been expecting it."

The students started coming in a few at a time. It wasn't long until the seats were all filled up and people still kept coming in and were soon lined up against the wall.

Johnny stepped up to the podium and said, "Good morning. Looks as if our class has grown quite a bit since yesterday. I guess it doesn't take long for the truth to spread."

There were giggles from the crowd. There were still some dissenting looks, but Johnny was sure that some had shown up just out of curiosity. He was also sure that he still had not convinced anyone that what he was talking about yesterday was the truth. Maybe today would be different.

"As I told those of you that were here yesterday, this is not your ordinary history class. I also told you that we were going to produce proof that the federal government had been deceiving each and every one of you in this room. Even the newcomers. Even your parents and your grandparents and even as far back as their parents. That's the reason that makes it that much harder for you to believe. I myself didn't always know the difference, but I was fortunate enough to be educated to the truth by a very special individual. That particular individual could not be here with us today. He has been gone for quite a long time. So in his absence, I have been instructed to deliver the message in his stead."

"Was that the ghost you were referring to yesterday, Mr. Gray?" asked one of the students.

There were several giggles around the room.

"Yes, as a matter of fact it is."

One of the students stood up and said, "This is ridiculous! There are some of us in this class that have been in the service and we served our country with honor. And you expect us to sit here quietly and listen to you downgrade our country based upon a concocted ghost story?"

There were murmurs of agreement going around the room.

"All I ask is that you hear me out. I, too, served my country and I feel I did it with honor to the best of my ability. But I don't feel that my country has treated me with honor. Not when all they have done is lied for the last hundred years. I told you I would bring you evidence of the truth and I have done that. So, if you would please be seated, I will present that evidence to you."

The young man returned to his seat, but Johnny could still see the anger in his face.

"This young man over here is Mr. Bobby Elmoe. He is a long-time friend of mine, but he also happens to be somewhat of a computer expert. Mr. Elmoe, Professor Livingston and myself recently went on an expedition of sorts. We had inside information of the great cover-up that we have been discussing. We had great success on this expedition. We have videotape of some of the things that we saw. We think that it is conclusive evidence. We also have computer discs of information on genealogical records, and historical records from all over the United States which were made long before anyone that is living today was born. These are records that the government has kept hidden from everyone for the last several generations. We also have plenty of the original records and books. And believe me, we're not stupid enough to not have all the backup copies that we could possibly need. So if after reviewing the evidence, you are not convinced or if you think this is

The Other Side of the River

some sort of a hoax, I will personally let any one of you escort me to the authorities. Now if you don't mind, Mr. Elmoe, would you please show us some of the footage on the video."

Bobby walked over to the table where he had the video machine set up. "Thank you, Mr. Gray," he said as he turned the machine on and started to narrate to the students what they were about to see. "These pictures were taken at an undisclosed location. It is undisclosed for obvious reasons."

Just as Bobby turned the machine on, the door to the classroom burst open. In walked Mr. Farnsworth, closely followed by two men in the black uniforms of the FPF or the Federal Police Force. Bringing up the rear was the student who had burst out of the room yesterday.

"Mr. Jones, are these the gentlemen that you have been so kindly telling us about?" Mr. Farnsworth asked the student.

"Yes, sir. I don't know who the other guy is."

"Professor Livingston, Mr. Gray, I believe these two gentlemen here would like to have a word with you."

The two officers approached the head of the class with their guns drawn. "Would you please put your hands behind your back?" one of the men asked Johnny as he removed his handcuffs from his belt and clasped them on Johnny's wrists.

The procedure was repeated to Professor Livingston and Bobby. "We are placing you under arrest for being a threat to the Federal government, conspiracy, trying to incite a revolution, possession of contraband material, and possible treason. The material in this classroom will be confiscated as evidence."

The trio was led out of the classroom and Mr. Farnsworth stepped up to the podium. "This is a fine example of what America is turning into. We will not tolerate such behavior. America cannot have such troublemakers in our society. We need more fine citizens like Mr. Jones here. Let's have a big round of applause for Mr. Jones."

The only one clapping was Mr. Farnsworth as the students gathered up their books and with their heads down, slowly left the room.

"Aren't we entitled to make a phone call?" Johnny asked the jailer, as the door to the cell was slammed shut behind them.

"Some people are and some people ain't." came the reply. "Depends on what you're charged with. And besides, it's not up to me. You'll have to wait and see what the judge has to say."

The jailer started walking down the hallway and turned around. "From what I've heard, I wouldn't count on it."

"Well, sir, would you be so kind as to give my wife a call and at least let her know where I am?" asked the professor as he handed one of his business cards through the bars.

"I don't see no harm in it. I'll see what I can do. Never did make much sense to me to lock people up without at least letting their families know where they're at."

"I certainly do appreciate your kindness, sir," said the professor as the jailer ambled on down the corridor to the door and disappeared.

"What are we going to do now, my boy?" the professor asked Johnny as he walked over and sat down on one of the three hard cots which was the only furniture in the room.

"I suppose we're going to have to wait and see how they plan on handling the situation. Maybe they'll give us a trial and maybe they won't. At least if they do, I hope they give us a chance to defend ourselves and to present our evidence."

"The only problem with that, Johnny, is that the more evidence that we produce, the more they have to use against us because the very evidence that we have is unlawful to possess."

"That's the chance that we're gonna have to take, professor. Hopefully, the evidence will be conclusive enough to convince the authorities of the truth and show them the absurdity of the laws to begin with."

"I hope so, Johnny." The professor stopped in mid-sentence when they heard the door down the hallway open up. The old jailer was walking toward their cell closely followed by a young lady who was carrying a briefcase.

"I got ahold of your wife, Professor Livingston. She's on her way down here and this here's your court appointed attorney," he said as he nodded his head toward the young lady. The jailer opened the door and let the attorney inside the cell and then retreated down the hall.

"Good afternoon, gentlemen. My name is Nellie McKeen. I've been appointed to represent you. I am the public defender for the Atlanta Federal District."

The professor and Bobby each shook hands with the lawyer. Johnny just stood staring with his mouth open. He was mesmerized with her beauty.

"Come on, Johnny. What's the matter, cat got your tongue?" teased Bobby.

"Oh, I'm sorry," said Johnny. "My name is Johnny Gray. I must have forgotten my manners there for a minute. This is Professor Livingston and Bobby Elmoe."

"I know. I have already looked over your files. I probably know more about each of you than you know about yourself. Let's get down to business," she said as she laid her briefcase down on one of the bunks, opened it up, and pulled out a stack of papers.

"The FPF has charged each of you with being a threat to the federal government conspiracy, trying to incite a revolution, possession of contraband material and treason. Any one of these charges could be punishable by life in prison or possibly even the death penalty. They seem to think that they have a very strong case against you. I haven't as yet seen the contraband material, but if it is as incriminating as they insinuate that it is, then it would be my advice, that you plead guilty and throw yourselves on the mercy of the court. If the material is not as incriminating as they say, or if you can convince me otherwise, then I think you should plead innocent. So what do you say, gentlemen? Do you want to tell me what we're up against?"

"What we're up against," said Johnny, "is almost a hundred years of lies and deceit. I will not go into that courtroom and plead guilty to charges based upon federally concocted misinformation. As far as I am concerned, we're not the ones that are on trial here. It cannot be singled down to just us three here. It's all the people. It's America itself!"

"Okay, okay, save the dramatics for the courtroom, Mr. Gray. You're going to have to get a little more specific if you expect me to help you."

"Just how specific do you wish me to get?"

"Why don't you start at the beginning? Don't leave anything out and be completely truthful with me."

"I'll be truthful, but I doubt very seriously that you're going to believe me until you get a chance to see what evidence we have."

"Let me be the judge of that. Just start at the beginning."

The door down the hall opened again, and the jailer showed Mrs. Livingston the way to the cell.

"Martha, I'm glad to see you," said the professor as he hugged his wife. "This is Miss McKeen. She is going to represent us."

"Miss McKeen, I'm so glad to meet you, but I must say that I'm afraid that you're going to have your hands full."

"I've only been here a little while and I'm already convinced of that," said Miss McKeen. "Come on in and have a seat. We're just fixing to get started. Mr. Gray was about to explain to me what led up to their arrest."

Martha took a seat on the bunk beside her husband and nervously twisted her hands in her lap until the professor reached over and patted her on the hand to calm her down.

Johnny started out his tale from the beginning when he was still a twelve-year-old boy and was awakened in the middle of the night by the old soldier. Miss McKeen gave Johnny a strange look as he continued his story.

Neither Bobby, the professor nor Martha had ever heard all of the details that Johnny was now telling. They were just as engrossed in the story as the lady lawyer was.

Miss McKeen was listening very intently without making any comment up to the point when Johnny mentioned Lige Nedpelter. Her eyes enlarged with a look of complete surprise on her face.

"Oh, my God! I can't believe this. You're not going to believe this. This can't be true!"

"What can't be true? Everything that I've told you is the absolute truth. You said that's what you wanted and that's what you're getting."

"Lige Nedpelter was the name of my grandmother's brother. He lived in Salt Lake City. He disappeared during the War of 2019."

"Did your grandmother ever mention anything to you about Lige owning a mule?"

Johnny could see that she was visible shaken, but she smiled when he mentioned the mule. Her face turned red as she laughed and tried to hide her embarrassment.

"You have a nice smile," said Johnny.

"Thank you, Mr. Gray," she said as her face turned red again.

"Why don't you call me Johnny and I'll call you Nellie. It looks like we may be spending some time together anyway?"

"Okay, Johnny," Nellie replied.

"We've got a diary which was written by Lige Nedpelter. I'm sure that you'll find it interesting."

"To tell the truth, I'm shaking inside right now. I just find all of this too incredible to believe. I don't know if I'll be able to represent you or not. I didn't realize that I would have a personal connection to this case."

"Anyone who is an American, anyone who has been deceived by the government has a connection to this case. Once you see the evidence we have on this, I don't think you will have any choice but to believe that we are telling the truth. I think that we can all agree that you would be the perfect choice to represent us."

"Here, here," said Bobby. "I'll vote for that."

"And I," said the professor.

"In that case, go on with your story, Johnny."

"After we got back to Atlanta, we studied over the material that we had accumulated to familiarize ourselves so that we could teach the people the truth. We realized that there could be dire consequences to this from the beginning. But we made up our minds a long time ago that it was just too big to let go. We are willing to do whatever it takes to get the job done. We don't want to overthrow the government. We just want the government to tell the true history and to admit that they made a mistake many years ago." Johnny paused. "There's just one thing that I would like to ask of you. Would you please not reveal the location of the vault or the repository that I've told you about? If we tell the location of those now, there is nothing that could stop the government from going in and destroying them. If we are successful in our case, then I have no problem with revealing the locations as it all belongs to the people in the first place."

"That seems like a reasonable request to me, Johnny, but I need to go look at this evidence if I am going to be able to defend you. And you have my word that I will not betray its location."

"Why I could take her and help her look," volunteered Martha.

"That's an excellent idea!" the professor exclaimed.

"Good, then I 'm glad that's settled," said Johnny. "Do you have any objections, Bobby?"

"No, it sounds good to me. Seems like we don't have much choice under the circumstances."

"Okay, then I guess I had better be going. I've got a lot of work to do. Mrs. Livingston, are you ready?"

"Yes, of course. But please don't call me that. Martha is just fine."

"Then Martha it is."

Nellie and Martha got up to leave and as Nellie pressed the button on the side of the wall to summon the jailer she said, "Oh, yes. By the way, the judge has refused to set bail, so you may as well get some rest and we'll get back to you as soon as possible."

The jailer came and opened the door and let Martha and Nellie out. Nellie couldn't resist a glance back over her shoulder at Johnny and the thought went through her mind, "He sure is a handsome devil." Then she scolded herself mentally for having such thoughts.

Nellie returned the following afternoon to report what she had found out. "The trial is set to start Monday. That gives me just a few days to prepare our case. Martha and I went by the apartment building and looked at the stuff in the basement. You can rest assured that if I ever had any doubts, they're all gone now. That material is just absolutely mind-boggling. I cannot express the importance of the historical significance and the implications that it represents."

"It's not just implications," said Johnny. "It's absolute facts. That's why it could not be ignored and we can't let it be destroyed."

"I know that, Johnny, but we have got to convince the panel of judges of that. I think our best approach will be to present enough evidence to the judges to prove beyond a shadow of doubt as to its validity. How can they prosecute someone with a clear conscience when the only crime committed was the pursuit of truth? I think we have a good chance of winning this."

Nellie and Martha spent the next three days looking over the material in the basement probing, searching, and learning all they could in the hopes that they could find a way to present this information convincingly to the panel of judges.

Finally, the big day came. Johnny, Bobby, and the professor were led into the courtroom accompanied by Nellie and three armed FPF officers. Martha was not allowed to go inside. The courtroom was empty other than the bailiff, as this was to be a closed hearing.

They sat down at a table in front of the courtroom and Nellie started explaining to them what she was going to do. "There is a panel of three judges. The first one is Richard Barnes from Trenton, New Jersey. The second is Nelson Thomas, who comes from Los Angeles, California and the third is Curtis Hines from Mobile, Alabama."

The bailiff stepped up to the front of the courtroom. "All rise for the entrance of your Honors Barnes, Thomas, and Hines," he announced as the judges entered the courtroom and took their respective seats behind the bench.

The first judge picked up a gavel and rapped on the bench. "You may be seated." After everyone had been seated, the judge continued, "I am Judge Curtis Hines. I am the senior judge for the Federal District of Atlanta." He indicated the man to his immediate right and said, "This is Judge Richard Barnes and the other gentleman is Judge Nelson Thomas. This court is now in session."

Judge Hines shuffled through a stack of papers that was lying in front of him. As he did this, he continued to speak, "As is normal procedure in a case where the Federal government is the plaintiff, it is not necessary to have a prosecuting attorney present as long as no bodily harm has been perpetrated by the defendant. The proceedings in this courtroom are being video taped to provide a true and accurate record. The decisions of this court are final and binding unless overturned by the president of the United States. Are there any questions?"

"Not at this time, Your Honor," Nellie replied.

"And who might you be?" asked the Judge.

"I am Nellie McKeen, sir. I am a new public defender for the Atlanta Federal Court District. I have been appointed by the local District Attorney's office to represent the defendants."

"Oh, great!" thought Johnny. "A brand new public defender. We're dead!"

"Very well, Miss McKeen," replied the Judge. "Welcome to the world of judicial process."

"Thank you, Your Honor," said Nellie.

"Would the defendants please rise?"

All three men stood up.

"The defendants, Johnathan Gray, Albert Livingston, and Robert Elmoe, have each been charged with being a threat to the Federal government, conspiracy, trying to incite a revolution, possession of contraband material and treason. How do you plead?"

"My clients plead 'not guilty', Your Honor."

"Very well. You may be seated."

The Other Side of the River

The three defendants and their attorney returned to their seats as the judge continued to look over the papers in front of him.

"We have in our possession a videotape showing the three defendants at an undisclosed location with what appears to be thousands of books and other ancient-looking machines which appear to be the forerunners of modern day computers. The defendants claim that these books contain historical and genealogical records of the American people. It is forbidden by federal law to be in possession of reading material that has not been approved by the federal government. According to this sworn statement by Mr. Thaddeus Jones, who is a student at the local university, the defendants were engaged, in his own words,

'… In the process of spreading preposterous lies as to the true history of the United States.' According to Mr. Jones, while attending what was supposed to be a legitimate American history class, Mr. Gray was telling a story about how a ghost had led him to the true history of what he termed as the War for Southern Independence. Is there any truth to this, Mr. Gray?"

"Yes, there is, Your Honor."

Charles E. Gist

"Truth to the story or truth that you were telling the story?"

"Both, Your Honor."

"Do you find it amusing, Mr. Gray, to fabricate stories to be told to students of history?"

"No, sir, I don't. Fabrications are what have gotten us into the situation that we are now in. My story is not a fabrication."

"Would you care to share that story with us, Mr. Gray?"

"I would, Your Honor."

Johnny related the story to the panel of judges, being very careful not to reveal the location of the vault, which contained records of the Church of Jesus Christ and the Latter Day Saints, nor the location of the branch of National Archives.

"Why is it, Mr. Gray, that during your narration you did not disclose the location of these alleged depositories?"

"Because, Your Honor, there is nothing that can stop the government from destroying these records and distorting history as they have done before."

"You are aware, Mr. Gray, that we have ways of obtaining information from uncooperative people?"

"Yes, sir. I am aware of that, but I am depending upon you being an honorable man and I hope that you do not have to avert to such tactics."

"Are you willing to disclose the locations?"

"When the proper time comes, sir, I will be more than willing. I would be happy to give you a private tour, sir."

"Thank you, Mr. Gray. How are you going to determine when the proper time has arrived?"

"When I have you convinced that what I'm saying is the truth."

"How do you plan on doing that?" asked the Judge.

"Excuse me, sir, but may I intervene?" asked Nellie.

"By all means, Miss McKeen. We didn't mean to ignore you."

"Thank you, Your Honor, but if you could give me an hours recess to retrieve some evidence, I think that I may be able to convince you that my client is telling the truth."

"Very well, Miss McKeen. It's getting near lunchtime. This court will recess until one p.m. tomorrow."

"Thank you, Your Honor."

The three judges got up and left the courtroom.

"What is it you have on your mind?" Johnny asked Nellie.

"There's only one way we can convince them that we're telling the truth. Now that we know who the judges are, I'll go look at the records and see if I can find out who their ancestors were. We'll play on their sense of pride."

"That's a marvelous idea," said the professor.

The three FPF officers came over and escorted the prisoners back to their cell.

After the recess the court was again called to order. Johnny could tell by the looks on the judges' faces that they were not happy.

Judge Hines slammed down his gavel and looked up from his papers with a scowl. "Do you hear that commotion going on outside this courtroom? There are people marching up and down the street and shouting for the overthrow of the government. It seems that someone released information critical to this trial on the networks of practically every computer in America. You wouldn't happen to know anything about this would you, Miss McKeen?"

"No, sir, I would not," said Nellie as she looked around at the defendants and saw Bobby quickly avert his eyes when she glanced at him.

"Well, let me assure you, Miss McKeen, I better never find out that you did. Mob justice will not influence this trial. This is a court of law and will be conducted as one. It is not a circus and I will not tolerate misconduct. It will be judged only upon the evidence and the pursuit of truth.

"I'm glad to hear you say that, Your Honor, because that is exactly what I am counting on," said Nellie.

"Then let us get on with the proceedings," said Judge Hines.

"I have here, Your Honor, information that I feel is pertinent to the case at hand. My clients are accused of several crimes against the government. It is my contention that it is not my clients that are guilty of wrongdoing, but the government itself that is guilty. You say that you seek truth and justice. That is also what my clients seek. You and all the rest of the world say you have never heard of the War for Southern Independence. Well, that is not surprising. Up until a short time ago, I myself had never heard of it. That's exactly how the government intended it to be.

Charles E. Gist

I have here, Your Honor, the records of three people. Perhaps under ordinary circumstances these would be three insignificant people. But these are not ordinary circumstances. I chose these three people for a particular reason and that particular reason was to make this situation personal. You will find in these files the genealogy of three men. A brief synopsis, if you will, of their lives and a list of their descendants. What do these people have in common? Why is it relevant to the case? The answer is very simple. Each one of these men had a common factor that affected their lives. That common factor was the War for Southern Independence.

I didn't just make these records up out of my head. Nor did any of my clients. If we had such vivid imaginations, I'm sure that we would be writing fiction books rather than following the vocations that we have chosen to make a living. If that were to be the case, we would not be here in front of you at this moment.

With your permission, I will place in front of each of you a file for you to look at."

"Permission granted, Miss McKeen."

Nellie placed a stack of papers in front of each judge. "I ask that each of you take a few minutes to

The Other Side of the River

look over the papers that I have given you." As the judges thumbed through the papers, Nellie continued, "The names on these papers may or may not sound familiar to you. If you look far enough through them, I'm sure that you will find some familiar names. Judge Barnes, have you ever heard of someone named Anthony Barnes?"

"Why, yes, I have. I have a nephew by that name."

"That's nice, Your Honor, but that's not exactly the one that I was referring to. If you'll notice, on the papers I put in front of you, they are labeled. Anthony Barnes. In April 1861, in Baltimore, Maryland, he was an 18-year-old boy who worked in his father's shoe shop. From that point on through May 1865, he was a private in the Confederate State's Army. He was a private in CO I of 9th Malone's Cavalry. Like I said before, if you will follow it on through the next few generations, you will find that this person was your own great, great, great grandfather."

"This is preposterous!" exclaimed the judge. "How do I know that these papers are authentic?"

"Oh, those papers aren't authentic. Those are just copies. I have the originals in my briefcase. But you can rest assured that the information you have in front of you is real."

Charles E. Gist

"How do I know that?"

"How do you know that it is not, sir? How do you know that the history of the United States that you have been told all your life is real? Have you ever seen any real proof?"

"No, Miss McKeen, I can't say that I have. But I can't say that I see any real proof to the contrary."

"That's my point exactly. I told you that I have the originals in my briefcase. The same goes for the papers in front of Judge Thomas and Judge Hines. If you have no objections, I would like for you to have these papers sent out to be analyzed to prove their authenticity through the process of carbon dating."

"I have no objection. Judge Hines? Judge Thomas?" The other judges indicated they had no objections.

"Bailiff, would you please take these papers from Miss McKeen and take them down to the laboratory to be analyzed?"

"Yes, sir, Your Honor," replied the bailiff as he received the papers from Nellie and proceeded out of the room and headed down the hallway to the lab.

The bailiff could clearly hear the protesters outside as he passed by Mrs. Livingston, who was sitting on a bench while nervously awaiting the outcome of the trial.

"Excuse me, sir, but could you tell me how it's going in there?" she asked.

"No, ma'am. I'm not allowed to discuss what I hear inside the courtroom.

"Oh, yes, of course. I understand," said Mrs. Livingston as she slowly sat back down on the bench and nervously crunched the handkerchief that she held in her hand.

"I can tell you this. I ain't never seen three judges look so nervous. You'd think they was the one's on trial."

"Thank you, sir, I think," said Mrs. Livingston with a faint smile as the bailiff continued his journey down the hallway and disappeared into a doorway.

About thirty seconds after the bailiff had exited the courtroom, Johnny felt a light tap on his shoulder and turned around and saw Uncle Jim sitting in the chair behind him.

"What are you doing here?" asked Johnny.

"Just thought I'd drop by and see how it's going. Looks like y'all got 'em on the run."

"Well, I don't know yet, but Nellie sure seems to be doing a fine job so far," laughed Johnny.

Johnny was brought back to reality with the rapping of Judge Hines' gavel. "Mr. Gray, would you care to share with this court what it is that you find so amusing?"

Johnny turned around and found that all eyes in the courtroom were fixed on him. "Well, no sir. I wouldn't."

"And why not, Mr. Gray?"

"Because you will probably think that I am crazy, sir."

"I thought you were crazy before I came into the courtroom, Mr. Gray. Now, would you please try to persuade me otherwise?"

"Well, Your Honor, you aren't going to believe me when I tell you."

"Try me, Mr. Gray."

"Judge, we're not alone in this courtroom."

"What is so hard to believe about that, Mr. Gray? Of course we're not alone in this courtroom. At the present, there are eight other souls present in this room besides you and I."

"There's one more, Judge. Uncle Jim's here, too."

"And who might Uncle Jim be?"

"He's the first one to tell me about the War for Southern Independence."

"I warned you that I would not tolerate misconduct in my courtroom. I will not tolerate a mockery."

"This is no mockery, Judge. I told you that you wouldn't believe me. You wanted the truth and that's what you got. Why not give me the opportunity to prove it to you?"

"Just how do you plan on proving to me that there's a ghost in this courtroom?"

"Ask him some questions."

"How am I going to ask questions to someone or something that I can't see or believe that even exists? How stupid do you think I am? Perhaps that last part of the question you better not answer."

"Let me ask the questions and we'll see if he's willing to answer them. You said you wanted the truth - now here's your chance to get it straight from the source."

"Straight from the source! I should hold you in contempt of court!" shouted Judge Hines.

"Don't laugh, Uncle Jim; it's not funny. He could probably add a few hundred more years to the sentence that I'll probably receive anyway."

"Just what does your friend find so amusing, Mr. Gray?"

"Judge, Uncle Jim says that this whole modern Yankee influenced society is contemptible and that he didn't expect you'd be willing to listen to the truth since you probably couldn't recognize it if it hit you up beside your big, fat, Yankee head."

"Big, fat, Yankee head?! Mr. Gray, I find you in contempt of court. You will be fined $1,000 for using language such as that in my courtroom."

"I apologize, Your Honor, but I was just repeating what was said."

"Well, you're still fined and tell your friend that he must refrain from such language if he is to remain in my courtroom."

"Yes, Your Honor. Uncle Jim said to tell you that he meant no disrespect and that he just got carried away there in the heat of the moment."

"Well, he should learn to control his temper. There are already enough hotheads in this courtroom as well as out on the street."

They could faintly hear the crowd outside in the background.

"Judge Hines, have you gone completely mad?" asked Judge Thomas, who up to this time had sat quietly taking all of this in. "Sitting here in a court of law carrying on a conversation with a nonexistent witness?"

"Yes, of course. I suppose I have. But do you have any other suggestions as to how we may find an answer to this madness?"

"Well, er, not really, but perhaps you've been working too hard lately. Maybe we should get someone else to handle this case."

"Nonsense, Judge Thomas, I wouldn't miss this for the world. So, come on, let's humor the man and hear what he has to say. You have got to admit that in all your years on the bench, you have never had the opportunity to converse with a ghost before."

"Well, all right, but not to humor him. I'll go along with it just to humor you. I still think you might consider a vacation or maybe even retirement."

"You may be right," the judge said as he faced in the other direction.

"What about you, Judge Barnes? I'm beginning to think that both of you may be crazy, but I've got to admit that it is intriguing if nothing else. Let's go for it and see where it takes us to."

"Good," said Judge Hines. "Mr. Gray, proceed with your testimony."

"Thank you, Your Honor. I'm not sure this is going to work, but I'll give it a try."

Johnny turned around with his back toward the judges and sat down on the edge of a table as he looked to see if Uncle Jim was still there. He was sitting in the front row of the courtroom with his feet propped upon the railing that separated the spectators from the participants in the court proceedings. Johnny turned his face back toward the judges and said, "Since I'm not a lawyer, I don't know if I'm doing this correctly or not. Should I have the witness take the stand or swear to an oath or something?"

"No, no, you go right ahead, Mr. Gray, just as you are doing. We seem to have veered away from the norm in these proceedings anyway," answered Judge Hines.

"Thank you, Judge," Johnny replied as he turned back around.

"Uncle Jim, can you substantiate that all the information on the papers lying in front of the judges on this panel is true?" asked Johnny.

"Now, dadgummed it, Johnny, you know good and well I can't!"

Johnny repeated the answer to the judges.

"And why is it that you cannot?"

"'Cause in the first place I ain't never seen those papers before and I ain't no recordkeeper on everyone that fought in the War for Southern Independence and I sure as heck didn't know all of them."

"I see," said Johnny as he repeated the answers to the questions as he would all through the conversation. "How are we going to convince these gentlemen that the subject in question ever occurred?"

The old man chuckled at that. "The subject in question? You mean the War?"

"Yes, I mean the War."

"Dadgummit, Johnny, maybe you did choose the wrong profession. You are starting to sound sorta like one of those lawyer fellers."

"Please just answer the question."

"Uh, what was the question again, Johnny?"

"How are we going to convince these judges that the War ever occurred?"

"Don't rightly know how we could convince these nincompoops of anything."

"Uncle Jim, I can't repeat that."

"Repeat what?" asked Judge Hines.

"Nothing, Your Honor, nothing important."

"What do you mean nothing important? If we are to have an accurate record of these proceedings, anything that is said I will determine as to whether it is important or not."

"He said that he didn't rightly know how we could convince these nincompoops of anything."

"Nincompoops?" The judge's face turned red with anger as he stood up.

"Sorry, Your Honor, but you asked what he said."

The judge sat back down and regained his composure. "So I did, and perhaps he's correct. It would take a bunch of nincompoops to sit here and listen to this testimony. Continue, Mr. Gray."

At that moment, the bailiff returned to the courtroom with the results of the test on the papers and handed them to Judge Hines. He looked at the papers, which were stamped and signed to show that it was a true and accurate reading. He handed the document to the other two judges to examine before he made any comment.

"It says here that the original papers have been carbon dated to be somewhere between two hundred and two hundred and fifty years old. That means that would make them somewhere around the mid to late 1800's. Which puts them into the correct time period into which you are implying. But that still doesn't prove that the so-called War ever occurred. I'm sure that even back then there was crackpots with vivid imaginations. Although, it does go on to say that the later pages do seem to be just as authentic chronologically as to the corresponding dates on the references of the people herein mentioned. That's very impressive, Miss McKeen."

"Thank you, Your Honor."

"Proceed with your questioning, Mr. Gray."

Johnny again faced toward the back of the courtroom. "Were you surprised at the results of these findings?"

The bailiff, who had returned to his position by the doorway, looked surprised. "Me?" he asked as he pointed to himself and looked around.

"No, not you, Mr. Greene. If you don't mind, please stay out of this and attend to your own job!" shouted Judge Hines to the confused bailiff.

"Sorry, Your Honor. I thought he was talking to me."

"Well, he wasn't. Go on, Mr. Gray."

"Okay, Uncle Jim, what can you tell us about the War for Southern Independence?"

"Like I said before, I ain't no recordkeeper. I can't sit here and tell you all about each and everyone involved. But I can tell you that it happened cause I was there. I was there when they was fighting at First Manasses and I was there when General Lee surrendered at Appomattox Court House and I was there in between. I saw many a good man killed and crippled up for life. And let me tell you it riles my dander up to see anyone denying that it happened. You got access to all those records that the government kept hid for all those years. They've already seen pictures of some of 'em. You know yourself, Johnny, that about the only way you're gonna convince these people is that you're gonna have to show the rest of it to them."

"I can't do that right now, Uncle Jim. I'm gonna have to be convinced that they won't be confiscated and hid out again or even worse, destroyed. We're going to have to find some way to convince them."

Uncle Jim sat there and scratched his chin. "Well, there is one other thing that might help out."

"What would that be, Uncle Jim?"

"Ask that gentleman there of the left if he happens to have a tattoo on his backside."

"Do what?!" Johnny asked.

"You heard me. Go ahead and ask him."

The Other Side of the River

Johnny turned back and faced the panel of judges. "Judge Barnes, Uncle Jim wants to know if you have a tattoo on your backside?"

"What! This is ridiculous. I don't have to tolerate such an imbecilic question from someone who is obviously an idiot. It is none of your business."

Judge Hines snickered. "Come on, Barnes, be a good sport. I'd like to know what it has to do with this case if you do have a tattoo on your butt."

Judge Barnes sat there red-faced and fuming, but he did not reply.

"Well," Judge Hines asked, "do you?"

"Yes," came the faint reply.

"And what is the tattoo of?"

"I don't know what it is. It's been there all my life. My grandfather was, so it seems, a practical joker. He had it put on there when I was a baby."

Uncle Jim walked over and whispered into Johnny's ear.

"What are you whispering for, Uncle Jim? No one can hear you but me."

"Just didn't want to take the surprise out of it, I guess. Go ahead and do what I told ya to do."

Johnny went over to the table and picked up an item and held it up so the panel of judges could see what it was.

Judge Barnes jumped out of his seat and shouted, "That's impossible! How do you know what's on my butt?"

"I didn't, Judge. Uncle Jim told me what to do."

"Well, if he knows so much, maybe he will be so kind as to let us know what that symbol stands for."

"I'm sure he would be glad to," Johnny replied. "Uncle Jim, would you please try and control yourself and stop laughing."

Uncle Jim was holding his ribs and trying to wipe the tears from his eyes. "I ain't seen nothing so funny since Cap'n Edwards got blisters on his butt and we had to soak him down in turpentine."

"Uncle Jim, come on, it isn't that funny."

"All right, all right, just give me a minute to catch my breath. Whew! Tell our Mr. Barnes that is the symbol of the greatest army that ever existed on the face of this earth. That is a symbol that is sacred to my heart and thousands of other fellers like me. That, my friend, is the Confederate battle flag and if'n everybody hadn't got so high and mighty the last hundred years or so, y'all woulda knowed what it was. Seems like your grandpappy musta been a mite smarter than what you are."

"That's ridiculous. I refuse to believe that bunch of nonsense," said Judge Barnes.

"If it's nonsense then you tell me what it is, Judge," said Johnny.

"Well, I don't know what it is."

"Does this picture look like your tattoo?"

"Well, yes, it does, but I still don't believe that concoction of yours."

"That is not a concoction of mine, Judge. I'm just telling you what Uncle Jim told me. And I suppose, Judge, that I concocted up all those two hundred-year-old documents and what about all the other evidence as you call it that was confiscated from my classroom? And I suppose in some way I was able to convey all this information to your grandfather. Your grandfather, Judge, out of all the grandfather's in the United States just so he could put a tattoo on your butt. Think about it, Judge. Maybe it wasn't a practical joke. Maybe he put the tattoo on you for a reason. Maybe it was something that meant something to him. Maybe you meant something to him and he left more to you than you realize."

The judge sat back with a sigh into his big chair. He didn't know what to say.

Judge Hines was the first to break the silence. "Would you care to place your tattoo into evidence, Judge Barnes?"

"Of course not," blurted out the red-faced judge. "This has been a long, tiring day. If there is no further evidence to be presented at this time, this court will adjourn until nine a.m. tomorrow. The three judges exited the courtroom and the three FPF officers escorted the prisoners back to their cell.

Nellie explained to Mrs. Livingston what had occurred in the courtroom.

"You mean this Uncle Jim actually exists?" asked Mrs. Livingston.

"If he doesn't, then Johnny sure put on a convincing charade," replied Nellie. "I have to admit that I was skeptical myself as to his existence, but now I'm not so sure anymore."

The trial continued at exactly nine a.m. the following day.

"Mr. Gray, do you plan to continue on the same line of questioning as you did yesterday?" asked Judge Barnes.

"Yes, sir, Your Honor, but my witness hasn't shown up yet."

"Perhaps your Uncle Jim doesn't know how to tell time."

"I don't think it's that so much, Your Honor. Maybe he just lives in a different time zone."

"Very amusing, Mr. Gray. Would you please inform the court as soon as your witness decides to appear?"

"Yes, Your Honor."

"Miss McKeen, do you have any further evidence that you would like to present to this court?"

"Yes, sir, I do," replied Nellie as she approached the bench and handed a document to the judge. "This, Your Honor, is a copy of what is called the Gettysburg Address. Abraham Lincoln, who was President of the United States during the time of what the northern states called the Civil War, wrote it. This document was written for the occasion of a dedication of a cemetery in Gettysburg, Pennsylvania, where one of the most decisive battles of the Civil War occurred. This battle took place in early July of 1863. It was known as the high tide of the war."

"Would you care to explain why, Miss McKeen?" asked Judge Barnes.

Charles E. Gist

"Yes, Your Honor, you see it was General Lee's plan to invade the north and inflict a crippling blow upon the northern forces which would further demoralize the will of the United States government to continue the War of Aggression on the southern states. He was also hoping to obtain recognition from Great Britain as to the existence of the sovereignty of the Confederate States of America. Unfortunately, Lee's army of Northern Virginia was defeated after three days of battle. Although after the battle of Gettysburg, the south never seemed to fully recover from the loss."

"I see," said the judge as he was looking over the document in his hand.

"Excuse me, Judge Hines," said Johnny. "It seems that my wayward witness has arrived."

"Then by all means, continue, Mr. Gray."

"Thank you, Your Honor. Do you have anything in particular that you would like to bring to the attention of the court today, Uncle Jim?"

"Sure do, Johnny. I see Judge Hines is holding a copy of the Gettysburg Address in his hand. Tell that feller on his left to look in his left breast pocket and see what he comes up with."

The Other Side of the River

Johnny repeated these instructions to the court. All eyes turned upon Judge Thomas, who seemed to look a little nervous as he was placed upon the proverbial hot seat.

"Judge Thomas, would you please do as Mr. Gray asks?"

"There's no need for me to look into my pocket. I know it's empty," said Judge Thomas as he placed his hand over his heart and his face showed a look of surprise as he felt something inside his breast pocket. "Why, what?" he stammered as he removed a piece of paper from his pocket and carefully unfolded it. "Where did that come from? I know there was nothing in there before I entered this courtroom."

It was an exact replica of the paper that Judge Hines was holding in his hands. Or was the paper that Judge Hines was holding an exact copy of the one that Judge Thomas was holding>

"This is impossible!" shouted Judge Thomas as he jumped up from his chair and stared at Johnny and dropped the paper from his grasp and it slowly floated through the air and landed on the floor in front of the bench. Just as the paper touched the floor, it seemed to disintegrate into a small red puddle, which appeared to be blood. All three judges were now out of their chairs and peering down at what used to be paper only a few seconds ago. Each and every one in the courtroom seemed to have lost the color from their faces except Uncle Jim, who didn't seem surprised at all.

The professor, Nellie, and Bobby were talking to each other as Judge Hines slammed his gavel down to regain order in his courtroom.

"What is the meaning of this, Mr. Gray?"

"I don't know, Judge, I didn't do it. I don't ever know what Uncle Jim is going to come up with next."

"Well, I have seen enough. I am tired of it. The time has arrived for a decision to be made. Miss McKeen, do you have any final statements that you would like to make to this court?"

"No, Your Honor."

"Mr. Gray?"

"No, Your Honor."

"Mr. Elmoe?"

"No, Your Honor."

"And what about you, Mr. Livingston?"

"Yes, Your Honor, I would like to make a statement before you make your decision. I am an old man and I don't plan to be around much longer, so it doesn't much matter to me what your decision is as far as it will effect me personally. I have been a teacher of history it seems for most of my life. I always tried to do a good job, but it saddens my heart to find out this late in life that what I've been teaching the young people has been wrong. I have seen the evidence, which has been discussed in these proceedings, and I know in my heart that every word that Mr. Gray has spoken is the truth. I think the time has come for modern man to hear the truth and to face the realities of the past to ensure the stability of the future. As the philosopher Josiah Royce once said, 'It is indeed difficult to define just who the modern man is and what views he has to hold in order to be modern.' Thank you, Your Honor, that's all I have to say."

"This court is adjourned until a decision can be made," said Judge Hines as he slammed the gavel and headed for the exit.

Three long, agonizing days of waiting, pacing, and wondering in the jail cell before the defendants were finally summoned to the courtroom.

"Would the defendants please rise?" asked Judge Hines.

Johnny, Bobby, Mr. Livingston, and Nellie all stood up in unison and faced the panel of judges.

"After careful consideration of the evidence presented during the course of this tribunal and a deep probing of our own conscience and consultation with the President of the United States, a decision has been reached. We find the defendants guilty as charged."

Johnny felt a knot tightening in his stomach and his knees becoming weak, as he physically had to fight to retain his balance.

"However, it is the decision of this court in concurrence with the President of the United States that all charges be dropped due to mitigating circumstances. But, Mr. Gray, you still owe this court $1,000 for contempt."

Johnny could contain himself no longer as he let out a rebel yell and grabbed Nellie to firmly place a kiss on her lips as he danced around the room to the silent echo of Uncle Jim, who was doing his own little jig.

Judge Hines firmly slammed the gavel down as he said, "Court dismissed!"

As the Judges were leaving the courtroom, Judge Hines placed his hand upon Judge Barnes' shoulder and said, "Now, about that tattoo of yours…"

Epilogue

"Come on and get your lazy butt moving, Private Gray. You don't have time to lay there sleeping all day. You got picket duty to pull and that goes for you, too, Elmoe," shouted Sergeant Nedpelter as he kicked Johnny on the foot to get him aroused from his slumber.

Johnny stretched to try to work the kinks out of his sore muscles that were stiff from the twenty-mile march they had made the previous day. He looked around in an attempt to get his mind cleared and saw that he was in familiar surroundings.

Bobby was scrambling to get his shoes on and get his gear gathered up to go and relieve the other soldiers that had already been on picket duty for the last four hours.

"You know, Bobby, I had the strangest dream. It had something to do with Colonel Livingston's daughter. What's her name? Nellie?"

"Yeah, her name is Nellie. I dreamed about her too, course that's not unusual as pretty as she is," replied Bobby.

"Yeah, but this was really a strange dream."

"Well, we don't have time to talk about it right now," said Bobby as he picked up his rifle and started walking off. "There's still about forty thousand Yanks on <u>the other side of the river</u> that we gotta worry about right now. You can tell me about it later."

Johnny grabbed up his rifle and trotted off after his friend.

"Yeah, I will, but let me tell ya. You sure ain't gonna believe it."

About the Author

Born in northeast Arkansas, the author moved to Florida during his first year of school. He has always been interested in history, especially Civil War history. From this interest stemmed a short career as a Civil War re-enactor with Company E 7th Florida, a membership with the Sons of Confederate Veterans and the authorship of a book of Civil War poetry, from the southern point of view of course. The author also has been working on his own family tree for the last twenty years. He graduated from Winter Haven High School in 1970. He is an industrial electrician by trade, the father of three boys and two girls and currently has five grandchildren. He moved back to his native Arkansas in 1996.

Printed in the United States
80889LV00006B/20